DESTINED TO Love

To willan Collier

Do Enjoy

Sally McGuire

DESTINED TO Love

SALLY MCGUIRE

iUniverse LLC
Bloomington

DESTINED TO LOVE

iUniverse books may be ordered through booksellers or by contacting:

iUniverse LLC
1663 Liberty Drive
Bloomington, IN 47403
www.iuniverse.com
1-800-Authors (1-800-288-4677)

ISBN: 978-1-4917-0021-1 (sc)
ISBN: 978-1-4917-0022-8 (ebk)

Library of Congress Control Number: 2013913278

Printed in the United States of America

iUniverse rev. date: 07/26/2013

To my son Neron who makes me believe
that I can do the impossible.

Special thanks to Carla Charles for always
having faith in me, Dianne Fortune and my
sister Nancy and the rest of the family.

Prologue

It was Friday afternoon, the end of the working week, and Akeila Morrow greatly anticipated the weekend. She and her two sisters had plans to visit the nearby island of Barbados; there they would go shopping at the most fashionable boutiques, relax at the spa, and party at the best night club on the island. There were books and papers on her desk that needed to be worked on over the weekend, so she neatly arranged them in a pile. Being an elementary teacher at the age of twenty-one was not what she had planned at that point in her life. However, she needed to save up enough money in order to pursue her doctorate in psychology. To become a psychologist was her dream, and she was very decisive in accomplishing that.

She looked at her watch and realized that she was behind schedule—her flight was in two hours, and she needed to get home and pack her travel bag. She quickly grabbed the stack of books and her pocketbook, which matched perfectly with her black velour pantsuit. She wore a white collared shirt that opened three buttons down, exposing a gold necklace, and five-inch black heels, which made her look taller than her five feet. While running down the steps that led to the entrance where her car was parked, a few of the papers and books fell from her hands, and before she grasped what had happened, she tripped and tumbled down the remaining four steps.

"Oh my God!" she screamed as the remaining contents in her hand scattered all over the concrete pavement. "Oh my God!" she cried once more when she realized that her elbow was bleeding. "Why did this have to happen to me now?"

She slowly pulled herself upward to a sitting position and observed her injuries closer.

"Are you okay, miss?" someone asked.

Akeila turned around quickly as a feeling of humiliation and embarrassment came over her. She thought that no one had seen her when she fell; all the kids had already left the school, and only a few faculty members were around, busily trying to bring their week to a end. Before she could answer, she felt strong hands under her arms helping her to her feet. She was still shaken and tumbled into the stranger's arms.

"Whoops! Steady now, miss. Are you sure that you are okay?" he asked again.

"No, I am not okay," Akeila whispered softly. "My knee and elbow hurt." Tears rolled down her face.

Che' Athien looked at the lovely woman standing in front of him, and her beauty took his breath away. She had the most beautiful brown eyes that complemented her round face and delicate jaw line. Her long, black hair was pinned in a ponytail with a few wild strands hanging at the side of her temple, exposing her slightly protruding forehead

"Please don't cry," Che' murmured. "Sit here." He led her gently to the step, and she sat down. "Let me have a look at your knee." He gently rolled up her pant leg. "That doesn't look good," he noted while examining her injuries. It was badly bruised, and a small amount of blood was visible. "I think that you should have it checked out."

"That is not necessary—it is only a bruise," Akeila replied. "People on the island get it all the time."

"That may be the case," Che' replied, "but these contusions can become infected and eventually will leave a scar. Do you want to have a mark on your beautiful skin?"

"Of course not!" she snapped, knowing that he was right. However, going to the hospital right now was impossible for her to do. She slowly went into her pocketbook and retrieved a small first aid kit, which she carried in case a student needed it. "Does this help?" she said as she handed it to him.

"It most definitely does," he said. "Now, let me take care of you." With skillful hands he cleaned and dressed the injuries on her knees and elbows. "All done," he said softly as the agony from her face disappeared.

For the first time, Akeila gazed closely at the guy sitting in front of her. It seemed as though he had done this before. He was remarkably handsome. His thick black hair was neatly cut, and his tanned face was clean shaven. He had a straight nose, well-formed cheek bones, and a strong, square chin. His muscular arms and chest were clad in a fashionable white Polo shirt, and Levi jeans and sneakers completed his appearance. His eyes was the blackest shade that she had ever seen, and as she looked into them she was spellbound. She felt safe and secure around him but could not understand why. "Thank you, Mr . . . . ?" she said, smiling while extending her hand.

"My name is Che' Athien, and you are welcome," he replied while taking her small hand.

"Thank you, Che'," Akeila whispered softly. She was shocked by her reaction when their fingers touched. Her heart was beating faster, and there was a warm feeling all over her body as she slowly freed her hand.

"Aren't you going to tell me you name?" he asked, smiling.

"My name is Akeila Morrow," she whispered, smiling once more.

Che' couldn't help observing how beautiful she looked when she did; her large brown eyes lit up, her dimpled face reddened, and she showed her white teeth. Her plum lips were shining from the bronze lip gloss that she wore. "You have a beautiful name."

"And you have an unusual one. Where are you from?" she asked, looking at him closely.

"I am vacationing here from England. The tourism brochure stated that Grenada is a great tourism destination," Che' explained, not wanting to get into the real reason why he was here.

"Are you enjoying your vacation so far?"

"Very much, I have traveled all over the world before, but not to the Caribbean. It is a wonderful place."

"Thank you again for all your help, Mr. Athien," Akeila said, looking at her watch. She couldn't believe how behind schedule she was. "I really have to go." With that, she rushed off.

"You are welcome," Che' replied, staring at her as she walked toward her car. She turned around quickly and waved as she got into her car and drove off. He stood for a minute gazing in the direction where she'd headed. She captivated him in a way that no woman have ever done before, and he wanted very much to see her again.

Two weeks had gone by since Akeila had meet Che' Athien, and she could not get him out of her mind. The images of his black eyes and the gentle way that he took care of her were constantly in her thoughts, although she tried not to think about him. She wanted desperately to see him again even though she knew that it was impossible, because he was probably backed in England. She was a silly romantic who had never been in love before, and she believed that when she did fall in love, she would know it.

The tropical island of Grenada had a temperature that was usually eighty degrees or higher during the day; at night it dropped down to around sixty degrees. It was surrounded by the ocean, and a refreshing wind cooled down the small island. Akeila would usually venture to a local beach that was close to her job, where she would relax after an exhausting day. There was nothing special about the telescope beach; it was underdeveloped and filthy, and coconut branches and litter were all over. The only beautiful part of the beach was its long, white, sandy coastline and the blue water. Over the years she had found an area at the end of the beach that she called her special spot. There was a big rock that was surrounded by a few shrubs and was shaded by coconut trees. The clean area had white sand and crystal clear water. She loves being there, away from everyone and the fast pace of life. She would sunbathe and breathe in the natural, clean smells of the ocean.

After a long swim one afternoon, she lay on the sand with her eyes closed, relaxing and listening to the normal rhythm of the ocean. Suddenly if felt as though the sun had disappeared behind dark clouds. Akeila opened her eyes slowly and realized that someone was standing over her.

"What the hell are you doing?" she screamed in fright, sitting upright and then quickly removing the sunglasses from her eyes. She tried to have a closer look at the intruder.

"Akeila, I am so sorry for sneaking up on you like this," Che' said softly when he realized that he had terrified her. He wanted to surprise her, but when he saw her lying there, he was spellbound by her beauty and stood motionless, staring at her.

"Che', is that you?" Akeila asked with uncertainty in her voice.

"Yes, it's me," he replied, smiling.

"You do not sneak up on a person like that! Are you crazy?"

"I am so sorry."

"You *should* be sorry!" she added furiously as he sat next to her on the sand. He looked into her big brown eyes and recognized that her anger was slowly vanishing. "What are you doing here?" Akeila inquired with surprise in her voice. She still could not believe that he was sitting next to her.

"I am here to take a sea bath and soak in some sun," he lied.

"Here on this beach?" Akeila replied with laughter in her voice.

"It is a beach, and it came highly recommended."

"Recommended by whom? Let me inform you that this beach is one of the worst on the island," Akeila said, still laughing. "Now, can you please tell me the real reason why you are here?"

"I love reconnoitering new and different things," Che'
replied simply.

"Oh really? Why do I get the impression that you are not
talking about the beach anymore," she said sarcastically.

"I have been looking for you and was informed that you
may be here," he admitted. "I wanted to talk to you."

"What do you want to talk to me about?" Akeila asked,
curiosity in her eyes, and then slowly she smiled at him.

Her smile took his breath away, and he was now fully
convinced that he had made the right decision in finding
her. He could not stop thinking about her. He remembered
vividly how vulnerable and helpless she was when he'd found
her lying on the ground. He wanted to take her in his arms,
to shield and protect her from everything that could hurt her.
She interested and intrigued him in a way that no woman had
before, and he was still astonished by those feelings. "I would
like to get to know you," Che' replied softly as he lowered
his eyes, staring at her almost naked body. Her leopard
bikini clung tightly to her petite, toned body, and its color
highlighted her brown eyes. Her flawless skin was shining
from the sun lotion that she had on, and her luscious lips were
so kissable that they made his groin tighten.

"Why? You are a tourist on vacation, and very soon
you will be leaving," Akeila said as she looked at him with a
puzzled, analytical look on her face. "Getting to know me is
not a good idea. And why are you gazing at me like this?"

"You are beautiful, and I am fascinated by you," Che'
said hoarsely, and she blushed. "I will be working on various
Caribbean Islands for the next few months, so I will not be
going back to England anytime soon."

"Oh really? What type of job would you be doing?"

"Training a special military unit that consists of a few
solders all over the Caribbean," Che' answered as he pulled a
twig from the sand and began playing with it.

"You've got a very interesting job," Akeila whispered as her
curiosity increased. "Are you married?"

"No, I am not," Che' said, smiling as he recognized that she was now showing interest in him.

"Why aren't you? You are handsome, educated, and hardworking."

"I may be all those things, but I still haven't found the right woman," Che' replied, stunned by her bluntness. He realized that she was very intelligent, and he loved that about her. He wanted to get to know her and was very determined to make it happen, so he cunningly changed his tactic. "How would you like to be my tour guide for the next few weeks? After all, school will be on break starting tomorrow." He smiled and then slowly took her small hands before she could give him an answer. "Let's go for a swim—the water looks refreshing."

Over the next few weeks, they were inseparable. They visited several cultural and historical sights on the island and sampled many local food and drinks. They leisurely strolled and held hands on the Caranage, the inner harbor that was the center of marine activities, and sometimes they watched the sun set after a long swim. They talked for hours about everything, and when Che' went to work on the different island, they wrote long letters to each other; he would sometimes draw cartoon characters to make her laugh. There was a force that was greater than the two drawing them together magically, and they fell deeply in love and could not visualize life without each other.

Six months later, in a small ceremony on the Island, Che' Athien and Akeila Morrow said their wedding vows before God and the Morrow family, promising to love each other forever. Two days later, filled with marriage bliss and hope for the future, they left for Woodstock, England, to begin their new life as husband and wife.

CHAPTER 1

It was the beginning of spring, and it seemed as though all of God's creation had suddenly awoken from a deep, long sleep. Birds sang as squirrels climbed in trees that had recently started to turn green. An early morning breeze blew strongly over Central Park in New York City. It was that time of the year when the park was always crowded. There were many different activities going on all around; some people walked and jogged, and others sat as children played happily. Everyone was very happy that the harsh winter was finally over. There had been fifty inches of snowfall, and at times the temperature remained constantly under twenty degrees. There were days when it was so brutally cold, that being outside even for a short period of time was considered be dangerous.

Akeila Athien sat on one of the numerous benches in Central Park. It was such a beautiful day that she wanted to enjoy it to the fullest, so she took the day of work and decided to go jogging. She wore a black sweat suit that fitted loosely to her petite body, and she had white Nike sneakers. Her long, black hair was pulled back in a ponytail, and the only visible sign of makeup on her lovely face was the bronze lip gloss on her lips. Large, black sunglasses protected her eyes from the sun as she observed her surroundings once more. A young couple caught her attention, and she assumed that they were newly in love. They were hugging and kissing as they stared affectionately into each other's eyes. Memories of the time when she first fell in love crowded her mind as she watched them. She quickly looked away and started jogging, slowly trying to escape from them. Over the past four years, she had done a remarkable job at stifling the memories of love, betrayal, and heartache. She could not escape them any longer—they came to her like a boxer receiving punches from his opponent . . .

Akeila arrived at Woodstock, England, with no idea as to how her life was going to change. The only sure thing was the fact that she and her husband were madly in love, and they were going to spend the rest of their lives together. The knowledge that Che' was no ordinary man had shocked her when she first comprehended it. They were greeted at the airport with armed guards who escorted them to a black limousine, and the men escorted them to his home. She was speechless when she saw his immaculate home. It was huge and designed in a modern style that portrayed elegant grace. Its interior was very luxurious and impressive. The decorative styles, which were different in each room, coordinated perfectly to match each theme. Even the furniture was made to look as though one piece grew from another. The rich, wooden floors were stained, and expensive rugs covered some areas. There were a number of paintings, some of which she'd never seen before. The house was perfect.

"Che', where are we?" Akeila asked, bewildered.

"This is our home, Akeila," he answered, smiling taking her in his arms. "Do you like it?"

"It's the most beautiful place that I have ever seen, but how can we afford it?" She looked into his eyes for answers. "Are you wealthy?"

"Yes, he is a very rich man, and a little nobody like you is not going to take advantage on him!" a voice replied.

Akeila turned around quickly to see who had spoken and was confronted with the most hateful eyes glaring at her. "Who is this?" she asked.

"Akeila, this is my mom," Che' said, looking at his mom with an angry glare. "Mom, this is my wife, Akeila."

"It's very nice to meet you," Akeila said softly as she extended her hand in greetings. She was trying very hard to compose herself in such an uncomfortable situation.

"What do you mean, your wife?" his mother inquires angrily, ignoring Akeila's outstretched hand. "Are you crazy? You went to work in those third-world countries, and you brought back a charity case, calling her your wife?"

"Mother, that is enough!" Che' shouted angrily. "Akeila is my wife, and I would appreciate it if you would show her some respect."

Akeila looked at the woman and was stunned by her offensiveness. No one had ever disrespected her in that manner before. She was always loved and appreciated by most people that came in contact with her; this kind of treatment was very unusual. Mrs. Athien was a very stunning and elegant woman. She was beautifully dressed in a designer turquoise pantsuit that fitted her tall, thin stature. She was around sixty years of age but looked much younger. Her long face was wrinkle-free, and her blue eyes were filled with resentment as they looked at her. Her long, white hair was fashionably pinned in a bun at the top of her head.

"You'd better get rid of her, son, or I will," Mrs. Athien growled as she frowned at Akeila.

"Let me make myself perfectly clear, Mother," he said harshly. "I love my wife, and if you continue to be so obnoxious toward her, you and I are going to have a very big problem."

"Are you threatening me?" Mrs. Athien challenged him.

"You can call it whatever you like," Che' warned, walking over and taking Akeila in his arms. "Your attitude needs some serious adjustment."

"I am so sorry for my behavior, son," Mrs. Athien whispered softly. "I was just surprised that you got married without informing anyone. What about Michelle?"

"Michelle and I have been over for quite some time now," he answered, staring affectionately at his wife. "Akeila is my

3

wife, and I would greatly appreciate it if you would try to be nice to her."

"I will try my best," his mother answered, smiling as she quickly wrapped her arms around them. Akeila look at Che's mom and knew that the woman was not genuine; even though Mrs. Athien was smiling at them, her eyes were calculated and mischievous.

Over the next few months, Mrs. Athien did everything in her power to make Akeila's life uncomfortable and miserable. Che' started a new job as chief of Homeland Security, and he was very busy working hard to prove himself to the government officials and the Crown. He would leave home early and came back late at nights, and on the few weekends when he was not working, there were many different things on the estate that needed his attention. The little time that they spent together was amazing, and every time they made love it was like a new experience. She knew that he loved her and did not want to burden him with her problems.

Her mother-in-law used that opportunity to be very unpleasant to her. She was verbally abused by her husband's mother in front of the servants and her friends. Akeila was branded a thief and was forbidden to venture in certain areas of the mansion; she was not welcome to dine or socialize with anyone. She would cry herself to sleep at nights and found relief by talking to her family members, who advised her on ways of coping in her situation.

She enrolled full-time at Cambridge University to occupy her time and was doing very well. She tried to adjust to her new life in England, but it was becoming too overwhelming for her. To be the wife of the chief of Homeland Security and a billionaire came with certain responsibilities that she was not able to honor. She wanted to be the perfect wife to him, but she wasn't given the chance to do so. His mother took care of everything for her son, from scheduling his appointments to making sure that his dry cleaning was done. Even though

Akeila accompanied him to parties and charity events, she still felt useless and incompetent. She didn't understand the social barriers and realized that the rich lived in their perfect little world, where she was not included.

The cold English weather was also hard to adjust to at first. Transitioning from tropical climate to winter could be very hard, but with her husband's help, she was able to adapt. He brought her the most expensive winter clothes, and she soon got to love the cold. Even though Akeila had these obstacles to deal with in the earlier part of her marriage, she persevered because of the love that she had for husband. The biggest distress of all was Che's betrayal, which she never imagined could happen. Upon finding out, she walked out on her one-year marriage with a broken heart. She never made any effort to contact or communicate with the man who had hurt her so badly.

Four years later, in New York, Akeila realized that thinking about the past was still very painful. With tears rolling down her face, she got into her car and drove off.

Che' Athien drank coffee from a huge mug. He had picked up the habit of drinking black coffee from his military life. Over the past four years, he had been introduced to government officials and members of the crown. With his leadership skills and experience, he had successfully solved some of the most high-profile cases, which made him one of the best operative that England had ever had.

He had been up since dawn, putting into action his plans for his latest assignment. Me made use of his brilliant team and was informed that there was a notorious man named Franko who was involved in drugs and human trafficking. That guy was very clever; so far they had not found any proof that could lead to an arrest. Che' knew that he needed to get some rest. He had gone to bed very late last night and only got two hours' sleep before waking up to do some work. Now it was evening, and he knew that he needed to get some rest.

Due to his lack of sleep, he started to have a terrible headache, so he slowly opened his desk draw and grabbed a bottle of pain pills, which he usually kept there. With eager fingers he quickly took two pills and swallowed them down quickly. He left the open bottle on the desk in front of him as he looked at his watch, and he decided to work for a little longer. As he was about to reach into his desk drawer to retrieve a folder, he knocked over the bottle of pills, which fell and spilled.

"Shit!" he snapped. "I do not need this right now." He began picking up the pills one by one and placing them in the bottle. While trying to find the ones that were stuck between papers, he stumbled upon a picture. He stopped what he was doing and sat back in his chair, gazing at the photo. It was a picture of his wedding day, which was the only visible memory of his failed marriage. Akeila looked gorgeous as she gazed affectionately up at him. Her long, black hair was pinned at the top of her head and was surrounded by a crown of beautiful white flowers. Her simple silk white dress was very chic and fit perfectly. White high-heel sandals, a pearl necklace, and earrings completed her outfit. Che' remembered thinking that he was the luckiest man alive when they'd said their vows. The honeymoon for two nights was at a beach cottage on the island, and it was one of the happiest times of his life.

He remembered every detail about the first time that they'd made love; he was very nervous and filled with great anticipation. The walls of the honeymoon chamber were painted, and the wooden floors were stained in brown. At the middle of the huge room was a queen-size mahogany bed that was covered with white silk sheets and matching pillows. On a small table close by, two bottles of Moet Champagne were chilling. The room had a breathtaking view of the ocean, and there was a balcony. He poured two glasses of champagne, lit some candles, and turned off the lights as he sat on the bed eagerly awaiting his bride.

When Akeila came to him, her beauty took his breath away. She wore short, white, lace lingerie and a matching bootie; her long hair fell loosely over her shoulders. She stood silhouette before him, waiting for him to make the first move. Che' knew that she was nervous because this was her first time making love, and he was going to make it very special. He took the wineglasses and filled them up with champagne, and then gently placed a glass to her lips as she drank timidly. He took her fingers and brought them to his lips, kissing the delicate skin on the back of her hand as she gasped and shivered. Her fingers found the back of his head as she ran her fingers through his hair. He then placed the wineglass down and sat on the edge of the bed before he took Akeila and placed her on his knees. He wrapped his arms tightly around her small body and buried his face in her fragrant, soft hair. He lowered his head to touch his lips gently against the hollow of her neck and felt her shiver some more. "It's okay, honey," he whispered. "We will go slow." Che' placed butterfly kisses over his wife's shoulders and then slowly moved to her neck. He head fell backward as he caressed her. He then sought her small, round breasts, and she moaned while he nibbled and sucked. Her nipples stood erect as he pleasured her, and she clung to him. He moved away a little and began undressing her slowly, and then he lowered his mouth and kissed her passionately. He gathered her against his body and laid her gently onto the soft bed.

Akeila caressed his muscular back and upper arms, sliding her fingers against his hairy arms, and then she stroked his nipples and felt them harden. His breathing deepened as he allowed her to curiously explore his body, enjoying her touches as his desire for her ripened. His hand traveled over her tights and then caught the skimpy underwear, which he pulled slowly off her body. There was nothing hurried about his movement. When she was naked, he laid her gently on the bed and elevated his body over her, so that his lips could nibble on her breasts once more. She groaned as his hand trailed down her stomach and then between her legs, which spread apart, giving him easy access. His fingers stroked and caressed the center of her needs until he found moisture gather at his fingertips. Che' replaced his fingers with his tongue, and her hips move upward as her area became extremely wet. She gasped, holding unto his head as he began stroking again with fingers that seemed to know exactly how to touch her. "Che'," she moaned as passion overwhelmed her. He quickly removed the rest of his clothes, positioned himself above her, and plunged into her. "Che'!" she cried at the first pain of entry.

He closed his eyes as his passion climbed to greater heights, and then he froze with pleasure as his self-control began to shatter. He knew that he was going to climax soon, and he wasn't going to let that happened. This was his wife's first time, and he had to put her needs first. "Are you in pain, honey? Do you want me to stop?" he asked her.

She reassured him that she did not want him to by wrapping her legs around his waist. Her hips lifted as he plunged deeper and deeper inside her, and they both cried out in ecstasy when he drove his final thrust of release. After making love to Akeila, he remembered gently cleaning her inner thigh with a wash cloth and warm water. She lay there smiling, and her big brown eyes stared at him with love.

"You are the perfect lover," she said, smiling at him.

"You, my dear wife, were everything that I expected and so much more," he replied, and he bent over and kissed her lightly as he cleaned and soothe her. When he was finished, he was shocked when she pulled him down to the messy bed, and her small hand found his buttocks and squeezed. Che' gasped as she slid one hand over his sex and caressed it, her fingers closing around his now growing erection. He moved to his back feeling pleasantly surprised as he gave her easy access to his body. To his amazement, her mouth replaced her fingers, and he groaned.

"Does that please you, my darling husband?" she whispered while smiling shyly at him.

"Do it again and please me some more," he replied, breathing deeply. "If you please me any more, I will explore." He lifted his head, bringing their faces together in a long kiss.

Che' positioned Akeila quickly over his hips and lowered her body until he entered her. She cried out as he held her hips. She then rose to her knees and lowered herself unto his hardness, moving her hips rhythmically. She eased from him slowly at first, over and over again. Then she lowered her breasts against his chest and increased the tempos of her movement. She rode him until they began to tremble, and as they cried out his body was shaking with sexual fulfillment. "I will love you forever, Che' Athien," she promised.

Che' walked over to his wine cooler, poured himself a glass of French vodka, and drank it quickly, not even conscious of its burning sensation. The study, like most rooms on the estate, was of fashionable design. A huge mahogany desk was extant at the middle of the room and contained numerous drawers, and a computer, telephone, and globe sat on top of it. There were four matching chairs that he and his business associates would use anytime he had to work at his home. A vintage cherry wine cooler offered two independent control zones; one kept the wine accessories and the other contained the wine at normal temperature range. A coffee table was the only other furniture present in the room. He slowly strolled over to his office window and gazed outside, where there was a direct view of the garden. The gardeners had done an exceptional job of beautifying the huge acre of flowers. The welcome sights of early blooming in a bed of crocuses, daffodils, hyacinths, shrubs, and wildflowers were all over. Spring was underway, and the various shades of colors gave the atmosphere a need to celebrate life.

Che' did not feel like celebrating anything. Instead, there was confusing emotion running through his mind. He could not stop thinking about Akeila, and he could not understand why she'd betrayed him. She had hurt him in a way that no woman had ever done before, and he hated her for that. Four years had gone by since she stole a million pounds from him and run off with her lover. After getting over the shock and betrayal, he had buried himself in his job and even got engage. The day that she left him was the saddest day of his life, and he remembered it quite vividly. He had come home very early from work wanting to celebrate his biggest fraud case conviction with his wife. The millionaire Erect Lewis was convicted of one hundred counts of fraud and was sentence to life in prison. Che' had worked very hard and made lots of sacrifices to secure that conviction. When he got home that day, she was gone and left a cowardly letter to explain why. It stated that she had never loved him and that she had found someone who had taught her how to love. Those words had hurt him for months, and they still did anytime he thought about it. His mom was happy to confirm that Akeila had left, and she got rid of any trace that Akeila had ever lived on the estate. Her clothes and personal belongs that she had left behind has been given to the Salvation Army. *Why didn't I see the signs?* he often wondered. He tried getting some answers from her family in Grenada and was rudely informed by her sister Pam that the money that was stolen was payment for a miserable marriage. The pain after that was so overbearing that he never tried to find her.

As time passed the heartache and pain turned into animosity and resentment. He'd thought that she was happy being his wife and partner, but he was wrong. Instead, she chose another, and they were living together and happily spending his money. The thoughts of Akeila making love to another man always put a jealous rage in his heart. Not being mindful of what he was doing, he forcefully threw the glass and its contents against the wall. "Shit!" he said angrily, and he began pacing the office floor. Why was he letting Akeila get to him like this? He thought that he had gotten oven her, but he realized that was not true. After seeing their wedding picture and reminiscing about the past, it awoke feelings in him that he had tried desperately to forget over the years. He had to find a way to get Akeila out of his mind and out his heart once and for all, and he knew exactly what he had to do.

A sudden banging on his door, intercepted his trend of thought. "Who is it?" he said angrily to the intruder. He had left specific instructions with his butler that he did not want to be disturbed.

"Che', it's me," a woman said. "Open this door at once!"

Che' walked over to the door and reluctantly opened it, and his fiancée stormed in. He was tired mentally and physically and wasn't in the frame of mind to deal with Michelle and her triviality. They have been engaged for the past two years, and she was constantly pressuring him to set a wedding date. He had no intention of marrying her anytime soon; after all, this engagement had been his mother's idea. Six years ago they'd dated, and after proposing to her, she bluntly turned him down. He was disappointed at first because they had so much in common: they had the same educational and cultural upbringing, and they socialized with the same circle of friends. She would make a perfect hostess, and his mother adored her. Shortly after that, however, he met Akeila, who became his all.

"I have been knocking for the past five minutes," she said furiously, looking directly at him. "Why didn't you open the door?"

"Sorry, but I did not hear you," Che' replied, already bored with his company. "I am very busy right now. How can I help you?"

"I have been calling your phone and leaving several messages. When you didn't call me back, I became very worried," Michelle answered as she curiously observed her surroundings and then focused her attention on the broken pieces of glass. "What is going on in here?"

"I had an accident," Che' replied as he went and poured himself another glass of liquor. Even though his headache had subsided, he was very tired and desperately wanted to go to bed. He then looked at his fiancée, who was a very beautiful woman. She was one of the best models in England and had graced the front pages of many magazines all over the world. Her tall stature and thin waist made her look like the typical model; however her waist-length blonde hair and deep blue eyes made her beauty striking. She was fashionably clothed in a short black Stella McCartney dress and matching high heel booths. Her long, beach-blonde hair fell neatly over shoulders, making her perfectly made up face and blue eyes very noticeable.

"Oh really? Well, we need to talk," she said bluntly, dismissing all inquiries of the broken glass.

"What do we need to talk about?" he answered, already aware of the topic.

"Che', darling, we have been engaged for two years." She smiled at him. "Don't you think that we should set a wedding date?" Michelle looked at the handsome man across the room and was determined to be his wife. When he had asked her to marry him years ago, she did not know his net worth, and so she turned him down. Her job took her all over the world, and being in the company of wealthy men and enjoying their resources was more appealing than being the wife of a military man. When she found out years later that he was a billionaire, he was already married to Akeila and it was too late. Akeila—oh how she hated that woman. "All our family and friends are eagerly awaiting our nuptials. I think that we should get married in the fall," she concluded.

"I am not ready to get married, Michelle," he replied as his anger rose. When his mother suggested that they get engaged for the good of the family, he'd agreed. After Akeila broke his heart, he vowed never to fall in love again, so an arranged marriage was very convenient to him. Michelle would be the perfect madam of the estate and would manage its affairs exceptionally. He had given up the dreams of having kids when he saw that Michelle did not possess any maternal qualities. His mother adored her, and he could not understand why. Michelle was proud, spoil, and selfish, and there were times when he loathed being around her. However, she was very passionate in bed, and he enjoyed making love to her—and a few of the other women that he had on the side.

"What do you mean that you not being ready to get married?" she asked with surprise in her eyes. "I am forty-two years old, and marriage is the natural thing to do."

"I thought that we were enjoying each other's company," Che' answered inattentively as he gazed at his office clock. It was already past dinner time, and even though he was not hungry, he desperately needed to go to sleep. During the many hours that he has been working, the maids had brought in breakfast and a light lunch, which kept him satisfied. "And you, my dear, have all the advantages of being engaged to me."

"Do you think that's all that I want?" She looked at him with incredulity. She enjoyed spending his money, the expensive gifts, the trips, and accompanying him to dinners and fancy parties—but she wanted more. She craved unlimited access to everything that he owned. She wanted to be financially stable, and it was going to take a lot of money to make that a possibility. At her age, the modeling jobs had become less frequent, and most of her saving had been exhausted. Being Mrs. Che' Athien was a necessity, and she was certainly going to make it happen. "I want to get married at the end of the year, and your mom think it's a good idea," she blurted out childishly.

"Let me make myself clear," Che' said furiously as he stared steadily into her blue eyes. "No one, not you or my mother, is going to tell me what to do. I will get married whenever I am ready!"

"Che' I am—"

"If you cannot understand or accept my conditions, I think that it's best that we call this engagement off!" he concluded, irritably punching his desk and scattering its contents.

"I do not want to call it off, honey," Michelle said tranquilly when she realized that he was furious. Calling off their engagement was the last thing that she wanted to happen. She quickly realized that changing her approach was the crafty thing to do in order to get him to marry her. Consequently she slowly reached out and kissed him hard on his lips. At his lack of response, she was more determined to seduce him, so she placed kisses all over his face and neck as she ran her fingers through his hair.

Che' remained motionless, scrutinizing the picture that was now visible on his desk. When Michelle started to unbutton his shirt, he gently pushed her hands out of his shirt and took a step backward. Her tricks were not going to work on him right now, because his thoughts were of Akeila. "I am very tired and need to get some rest," he said softly, trying not to hurt her feelings.

Michelle was very confused. Since they'd gotten back together, Che' had never passed on making love to her. *What is wrong?* she wondered, when the picture on the desk caught her attention. "Whose picture is this?" she questioned innocently, reaching out and taking it.

"Give it to me," he said calmly.

"Why? Let me look at it," Michelle replied, smiling. When she looked at the picture, her expression changed. "Your wedding picture!" she screamed, staring at Akeila with hatred and contempt. From the first time that Michelle had seen her, she hated her, and the animosity seemed to grow anytime that she heard her name or saw anything reminded her of that woman. "Why do you still have this? Is that the reason why you do not want to marry me?"

"Give me my picture," Che' replied calmly as he extended his hand.

"You want it? Here!" She tore the picture in two pieces.

"Why did you do that?" Che' said infuriated as he snatched the pieces from her hands. "You have no right to come to my home and destroy my property." He looked at her with anger blazing in his impenetrable black eyes and said quietly, "Get out!"

Michelle was baffled by Che' behavior and was even more confused by his reaction to the picture. As she looked at him and saw how angry he was, she was convinced that he was still in love with Akeila. The realization pierced her heart like a sharp knife, which fueled her anger even more. After all the hard work that she had put into destroying his marriage and becoming his new bride, she was not going to lose now. She was going to do whatever it took to be the next Mrs. Che' Athien.

"You are such a fool, Che' Athien!" she yelled, walking toward the door. "After all the pain and humiliation that bitch put you through, you are *still* in love with her." Michelle looked at him when he did not answer. He stood there angrily glaring at her with a lethal expression on his face. She had never seen him so mad before, and it startled her. "Akeila is gone, and you should accept it so that we can move on with our life," she added before she walked out of the room.

Che' took the torn picture, securely placed it in his pocket, and then went to his bedroom. He quickly showered and then went to bed. He fell asleep moments later with his mind crowded with thoughts of Akeila, as he thought of ways to get her out of his heart once and for all.

Franko Lewis sat in the black booth alone at the elegant, expensive pub in East Woodstock. He was meeting with his contact at Homeland Security, who kept tabs on Che' Athien. There was not any valuable information available, and that had the case for the past four years. He despised Che' Athien and desperately wanted to destroy him. The task was more difficult than he had anticipated even though he had connections all over the world. His adversary was well protected by the best security team. His home was under twenty-four hour surveillance, and one had to have an appointment to visit there. Franko's research had proven that

Che's grandmother had left all her worldly possessions to him, making him a billionaire at a very early age. Franko hated rich people, and one in particular: Che' Athien. He had taken from him the only family that he had ever had, and Che' was going to pay dearly for doing so. Franko took a last mouthful from the glass of bourbon that he was drinking and ordered another.

The memories of his miserable childhood haunted him from time to time. His mom, a single mother of two, did everything in her power to ensure that they had a good life. After dating a string of losers, she fell in love and married Laurie, a local banker. She thought that she would finally give her boys, nine and twelve at the time, the type of life that they deserved. Little did she know that Laurie was a drunk and an abuser. Anytime he was drunk, he would verbally and physically abuse the three. His mom was fearful of him and was too weak psychologically to leave. The only person who tried to protect him was his older brother, Erick. Even though Erick was only three years his senior, he idolized his brother, who taught him how to play baseball and fight off bullies. There were times when his stepfather would be beating on him or his mom, and Erick would step in and take the thrashing instead. His brother made life tolerable and sometimes happy in such an unhealthy environment.

After dealing with the abuse for five years the brothers had had enough. Franko remembered clearly the incident that happened on a fall night and changed their lives forever. He and Erick had come home from a school baseball game, where Franko had scored a home run. The teenagers were filled with excitement and wanted to share the good news with their mom. When they entered the house, they found her curled up in a corner with a blooded eye and a busted mouth. Their stepfather was standing over her with a beer bottle in his hand, examining her. On impulse Franko took the baseball bat that he was carrying and hit Laurie forcefully behind the head; the drunk fell to the ground. The two brothers punched and kicked his body until it was lifeless. When the three noticed that he was dead, they took his body and threw it in a swamp nearby, vowing to keep that secret until death. The body was never found, and the death was considered an unsolved mystery.

From that day their lives change for the best. Laurie had a large sum of money saved up, and his mom was the benefactor. When they graduated from college, His job choice was different: he did whatever he could to make a quick dollar, and he made a name for himself. Erick went into investment and was very good at it . . . until Che' Athien investigated and convicted him for fraud. His brother was sentenced to one hundred years in jail, where he later committed suicide. Franko's vengeance escalated even more when his mom died of a heart attack three months later due to the stress of losing her son. He vowed on their graves that he would not rest until he'd had his revenge.

Franko took another drink as he scanned his surroundings. The pub was a perfect Georgian style with Victorian décor. There were video cameras and a bouncer, who blended in with the people. Everything in the room was elegant and of high quality, from the tables and chairs to the drinks and food. The wealthy socialized there, and sometimes he would find himself enjoying their company, especially the women. He loved beautiful women and was very confident of his skill at charming them. He took a final drink from his glass and got up to exit the pub when he noticed a beautiful blonde enter. Her ambiance captured his attention, and he could not take his eyes away from her. She seemed angry as she marched into the bar, ordered a beverage, and downed it.

He walked over to the bar, sat next to her, and ordered a drink. "Good evening, can I offer you a drink?" he asked. The woman rudely disregarded him. He was accustomed to dealing with rich, spoiled women who thought that he was beneath them; however, this one interested him. He was going to do whatever it took to have her in his bed tonight.

Michelle drank her fourth glass of French vodka, still ignoring the stranger. After years of partying and drinking, it took a very large quantity of alcohol to get her intoxicated. She was not concerned about the amount of drinks that she was having; all she wanted was to drown any thoughts of Che' and Akeila from her mind.

"Can you believe that he is still in love with her?" she said suddenly, looking at the stranger for the first time. He was not a bad looker; he was ruggedly handsome and had a dangerous gleam in his blue eyes.

"Who is?" Franko asked, pretending that he was concerned about her problems. He got an opening and knew that it was only a matter of time before she left with him.

"My fiancé. He is still in love with his ex-wife." She took another drink as anger blazed in her eyes.

"I am so sorry to hear that," he said sympathetically. "It is very hard to believe that any man could resist your charisma. You are a very beautiful woman."

"My name is Michelle," she said, smiling seductively at the stranger and knowing the effect that she had on men. Her slender stature, long blonde hair, and blue eyes made her look like a Barbie doll. She craved attention from men and loved when they complimented her.

"It's a pleasure to meet you, Michelle," Franko replied, smiling as he extended his hand in greeting. "My name is Franko."

"Franko, can you imagine that he was not interesting in kissing me like this?" Michelle whispered as she kissed him deeply on his lips. Even though he was astonished by her impulsiveness, he gladly kissed her back. Her tongue taste like vodka, but it was not of any importance to him, because the kiss created shockwaves in his lower body. "It's because of that bitch!" she added quickly, pulling away from him.

"Oh? Do you really think that is the reason why he did not kiss you back?" Franko was uninterested in the conversation.

He wanted to continue what she had started when she kissed him. "Let's get out of here," he whispered in her ears.

She smiled at him in compliance. "For someone who is extremely intelligent, he can be injudicious," Michelle added bitterly as she got up and held on to Franko's arm. This situation was not foreign to her; tonight she did not want to be alone, and the stranger seemed like an enjoyable companion. As they exited, she added, "People think that he is the great and powerful Che' Athien. Please!"

"What did you say?" Franko asked, stunned at the coincidence.

"I only said my fiancé's name, Che' Athien," she said as she got into the front seat of the car. Franko remained speechless as he got in and drove off with a victorious smile on his face.

CHAPTER 2

I t was approximately four o'clock when Akeila finished all of her chores. She did the laundry and neatly put it away, cooked dinner, and cleaned her cozy two-bedroom apartment. She needed to leave in a few minutes in order to keep her appointment. She quickly dressed into a pair of skinny black jeans, a red turtle neck sweater, and flat boots. Then she applied some light makeup, grabbed her pocketbook, and headed to the door. She looked around the apartment once more and was very satisfied: everything was cleaned and neatly arrange. There was a small, wooden table situated in the middle of the leaving room on top of a white peace of sheepskin; it synchronized perfectly with the three pieces of furniture: a brown leather loveseat, a white recliner, and a brown wooden wall unit. Most of the floors were stained with brown except the bedroom area, which was carpeted. The few pictures hanging on the white walls and the curtains in the windows gave the apartment a very homely feeling.

Akeila drove her Jeep through the busy Eastern Parkway traffic, turned on Church Avenue, and double-parked in front of Don Carlos Preschool. There was always a problem finding a parking space there, so she quickly ran inside the building, hoping that the traffic police would not pass by. When she got in the classroom, she saw him sitting at a table coloring a picture, and her heart was filled with pride. Her three-and-a-half-year-old son, Link, was her pride and joy.

He looked up and saw her walking toward him, and he ran into her outstretched arms. "Mommy, Mommy!" he cried.

"Good afternoon, Link," she said, kissing his chubby cheeks. "We have to leave quickly—Mommy is double-parked."

"Okay, Mommy," he answered as they took his personal belongings, said good-bye to the teachers and other kids, and left the building.

"How was your day today, honey?" Akeila asked as she strapped him in his car seat before driving off.

"It was okay, but Austin did not want to share with me."

"That was not nice," she said, looking at the frown on his small face in the rearview mirror.

"I know, Mommy—I always share," Link said proudly as he took the toy plane from the car seat and starting playing with it. This was his favorite toy, and she always made it accessible so that he could find it whenever he wanted to play.

"That's my boy!" Akeila replied, smiling. He had brought so much joy in her life, and she could not imagine her life without him. He had given her motivation to works toward her dreams in order to make a good life for the both of them.

"Mommy, can I have some chicken nuggets and fries, please?"

"Okay, my love. After I get you the food, we are going to the airport to pick up your grandparents, Aunty Pam, and Tasha."

"Really? Am I going to see a plane?"

"Yes, you are, honey," Akeila whispered, looking at her son once more, who was smiling happily as he pretended to land his toy plane on an air strip. He had her smile, but that was the only feature of hers that he possessed. He was the spitting image of his father. They both had the same black hair, eyebrows, and nose, and their eyes were as black as night. From the moment she found out that she was pregnant, she became very protective of him. She ate healthy foods, took her vitamins, and never missed a doctor's appointment. When she heard his heartbeat and saw his sonogram for the first time, she cried tears of joy. From that point on, she would sing, read, and talk to him, telling him about his daddy. When Link was born, he was a healthy, seven-pound baby. Upon seeing his face for the first time, Akeila cried tears of delight because her love for him was so great. Then she cried more when she recognized how much he looked like his father. As the years went by, the resemblances grew stronger. The only minor difference was that her son's hair was curlier, and his skin was a shade darker.

She drove through the restaurant's drive through, purchased the food, and then handed it to him. Link started to devour it. "How is the food, honey?" she asked.

"It's yummy, Mommy. Are we there yet?" Link asked.

"Not yet, but we are almost there."

Moments later they arrived at JFK Airport, which was always busy. She saw people hurrying to and from their destinations. Akeila looked at the flight schedules and realized that her family flight was delayed, so she took the opportunity to take her son exploring through the airport. They visited a few gift shops, where she purchased a cup that had a little plane drawn on the sides, and then they had a Popsicle. Afterward they went to the waiting area, and when they saw a plane landing, Link beamed with excitement.

"Mommy, Mommy, look at the big plane!" he shouted happily as he pointed to it.

"Whoa, look at the colors, white and blue!" Akeila said, trying to sound as excited as her son. His love for planes started when her sister Pam bought him a toy plane for his second birthday, and every day it grew stronger. "Link, here comes the family," she said, pointing in the opposite direction. She was always happy to see them because they were a very important part of her life.

"Where, Mommy?"

"They are over there, baby."

"Grandma, Grandpa!" Link screamed, running happily into their outstretched arms. Akeila followed close behind as they hugged and kissed each other. From the moment Link was born, her family had been a huge part of his life. They were present at his birth and took turns babysitting him until he was two years old, while she went to school to pursue her doctorate in physiology. They never missed his birthday and called regularly to make sure that everything was well with them.

"How is the graduate to be?" her sister Tasha asked as they hugged once more. Tasha was the middle child and was wild and spontaneous. As a fashion designer, her job took her all over, and she was always fashionably dressed. Her hair was cut sort and bleached, and her face was perfectly made up.

"Can you believe that our kid sister has a doctorate in psychology, and she is considered a great shrink by the people that she works with?" Pam, her older sister, said with pride in her voice.

"I think that you are happier than Akeila," Tasha replied, laughing. "Anyone listening will think that you are the one graduating from graduate school."

"She is very proud of me," Akeila said as she kissed her older sister's cheeks. Pam worked at the local television station in Grenada as an anchorwoman, and she had been happily married for the past seven years. She'd met her husband, a pilot, when studying journalism overseas. She was very protective of her younger sisters and would always give them advice about how things should be done, even though at times they did not listen. As a journalist, she was very enlightened about the affairs of this world, and she wanted to safeguard them from anything or anyone that had the capability to create harm. She was always there whenever they needed her. Like the other Morrow girls, she was very gorgeous. She was of medium height and had the same round face and delicate cheekbones as her sisters.

"We all are so proud of you, honey," her father said gently as he took her hand and kissed it.

"Aunty Pam, did you bring me my present?" Link asked, taking hold of her hand.

"What present?" Akeila asked, looking at Pam.

"Aunty Pam called yesterday and asked me what I wanted, and I told her," the child replied.

"Pam, Link does not need any more toys," Akeila said with a scowl. "The last time that you all visited, you brought him enough stuff."

"Relax, Akeila. Let us spoil our nephew," Tasha replied, ruffling his curly hair as Pam held his small hand. "After all, he is the only baby in the family."

Akeila looked at how happy they all were and laughed. She knew how much they loved Link, and arguing would be a waste of time. "Let's get out of here!" she said with both sisters, taking hold of her son's hand. Her parents talk to him while they exited the airport.

The Morrow family was very proud, loyal, and loving. They were extremely close and could depend on each other at all times. When she found out that she was pregnant, they were her only source of strength and support. They showered her with love and were there for her while she tried to deal with her husband's betrayal, years ago.

Cambridge University was an excellent place of learning and offered a wide variety of classes. Akeila loved being there, and the place became her safe haven. She had been enrolled full-time there and even took courses during the summer and winter break, in order to quickly obtain her degree. Since her husband was always working and she did not feel comfortable at the estate, she was at the university as much as possible, volunteering and taking part in any extra curriculum activities pertaining to her area of study. It was during a lecture, in one of her summer classes that she remembered feeling very tired and fatigue. She thought that it was the hot weather and her lack of appetite that was contributing to that strange feeling. After feeling that way for a few hours without any change, she decided to go to the doctor. On her way to the doctor's office, her reflection caught her attention in the store front mirror.

She was baffled at what she saw: her huge brown eyes looked tired and lifeless, her skin was pale, and her petite body had lost some weight. *What's happening to me?* she wondered, staring at the stranger who was looking back at her. She knew that she was unhappy and had not been eating well. She then hurried to her doctor for a diagnosis, who informed her minutes later that she was already four and a half months pregnant. She was overjoyed and wanted to share the good news with Che', knowing how much he wanted to be a dad. He had expressed that desire regularly, especially after their lovemaking. With faith in her heart, she believed that a baby would definitely change their lives for the best. After going home to shower and dress, she went to his workplace for the first time, to surprise him. Unfortunately, she was the one who was shocked.

Upon arriving, she heard voices and did not want to interrupt, so she quietly stood behind the slightly open door and peeped in. There she saw Michelle sitting in her husband's lap as they kissed. They were so engrossed in what they doing that they did not observer her standing there with tears falling from her eyes. She ran from the building sobbing and vowed never to see him again.

"Akeila, did you hear what I just said?" Pam asked with a worried look on her face as they pulled up in front of her apartment.

"I am sorry, Pam. My mind was far away," Akeila whispered softly with a sad expression on her face.

Pam hated seeing her sister so unhappy. She knew who the cause of it was, and her anger intensified. "Akeila, you will be graduating in a few days, and you should be very proud of yourself. You are beautiful and are a wonderful mom," Pam said gently. She hated Che' Athien for all the pain that he and his family had put Akeila through. When Akeila told the family that they were getting married, Pam was the only one who'd objected to the marriage. She went along with the wedding because of the love that they shared, and she wanted to support her. When they left for England, she had sleepless nights worrying about her young sister, who was clueless about love and marriage. The saddest time of her life was when Akeila called her crying because of her unhappiness. Pam wanted to bring her home but knew that this was not her decision to make; her sister had to grow up and figure out what she wanted to accomplish with her life. When she left her husband while pregnant and with no objective, her family made all the necessary sacrifices to make the transition period as easy as possible.

After years of hard work and determination, Akeila could have the future that she was meant to have. They had all cleared their busy schedules so that they could be a part of her graduation ceremony. Pam wanted her to be happy and was proud of her achievement; that was the reason why she could not let her know that Che' had called a few days ago inquiring about her. There was no reason to tell, because the information would only bring up the past.

The view from the busy Brooklyn Bridge was breathtaking. There was a manmade waterfall connecting with the huge body of water under the bridge. Che' thought that the artwork was very unique and creative as he drove his rental BMW across the bridge. He was astonished when he saw a train pass in close proximity to where he was driving. New York was an amazing city, and everything that he had read about the place was true so far. The city that never slept was a very applicable name because there was something always happening. From the moment that he had landed, everything seemed to be moving at a faster pace. People busily rushed, whether they were driving or walking. The place had an energy that put one in tune with everything that was going on. It was early July, and the weather was much hotter than it was in England at that time of year.

Che' reached across the passenger's seat and retrieved a map of the city, placing it on the steering wheel and gazing at it quickly. He tried to locate the Surrey Hotel. When he realized that it was only minutes away, he decided to slow down a little and enjoy the scenery some more. He rolled the car window down and welcomed the summer breeze. He was casually dressed in khaki cargo shorts, a white polo T-shirt, and sneakers. His black hair, which had a patch of gray at the front, was blowing in the wind, and his eyes were protected by a pair of Ray Ban sunglasses. It was still mindboggling that he was in New York trying to find his ex-wife. Even though she had stolen from him and betrayed him, he still thought of her as his wife. He had never filed for a divorce, but his lawyers had drawn up the necessary documents in order for it to be done. Che' had no idea how he was going to get his revenge against Akeila for betraying and stealing from him. Morally she was not punishable by law for adultery, but theft was a crime that was admissible in court. That small amount of money did not matter much to him because he was a billionaire and was financially stable. However, he wanted her to suffer just a little for all the pain that she had put him through and the damage that was done to their marriage.

As he approached the hotel, he started having flashes of Akeila in his mind: her smile and the way that her brown eyes lit up every time they made love. He did not want to reminisce about their past—after all, it was bittersweet. Even though he pretended that she never existed in his life, he was always wrestling with his heart, which told a different story.

When he walked into the luxurious Surrey Hotel, it was everything that the brochure said that it would be. The lobby was filled with a collection of several works of art, which made the area look like a small museum. What made him choose that hotel above all the luxurious ones in Manhattan was its low visibility; he wanted to be at a place, where there was privacy and was not easily noticed, because his security guards were not present on this trip. He was welcomed by a beautiful, blonde receptionist who flirted with him while getting his room information.

Minutes after reaching his room, he took a shower, put on his robe, and sat on the bed with his laptop, strategizing his next move. He recalled the phone conversation between him and Akeila's sister Pam, and he smiled. She was very surprised to hear from him and made no effort to hide her resentment. When he informed her that his interest was only to inquire how Akeila was doing, she laughed ironically and proudly stated that her sister was doing great and would be graduating from Hofstra University in a few days with a doctorate in psychology. She then rudely hung up the phone without saying good-bye. He found the clue that he wanted in regard to where Akeila was. His resources indicated that Akeila had not left England by plane, and because she did not use her name, it was not easy locate her. As an agent he was very impressed by her brilliance in making it very difficult to trace her whereabouts. She had always showed interest in his job by asking many questions, and he was happy to answer. Che' googled Hofstra University and found its location and schedule for the graduation ceremony. He got up from the bed, took a drink of Grey Goose, and then got dressed.

CHAPTER 3

The commencement exercise at Hofstra University was a special occasion for the graduates and their families; it marked the culmination of hard work and studies, and everyone radiated with excitement. The audience was filled with families, friends, and faculty members who wanted to celebrate the experience. Akeila looked down from the stage at her family, who was sitting in the front row of the huge hall, and she smiled. They were the first ones to arrive, so they had acquired those coveted sits. They were impressively dressed as they talk among themselves. Her son sat next to Pam playing with the new toy that she had brought him, and he was still beaming over it. The plane was small and beautifully crafted; it was made out of mahogany wood and had his initials written on it. Link was overjoyed when he received it, and he even slept with it on his bed. Over the past few days, the family had visited the museum of Natural Arts and the Madame Toussauds Wax Museum; they were greatly amazed at everything that they saw. They did a lot of shopping for some of the things they needed to take back home once their short trip was over.

The hall was now filled to capacity as the ceremony commenced. The valedictorian and dean gave their speeches, and then the choir sang. Finally it was time for giving out the diplomas, and the mayor of New York handed them to the graduates. Akeila walked gracefully across the stage when her name was called. When she received hers, she smiled at her family, who stood up to cheer and take pictures. She looked at them once more and then fixated on her son. She was very ecstatic because one of her dreams had come true. Now she could find a better job and would be able to provide for her son. She returned to her seat with pride and happiness in her heart.

Che' sat in the back of the crowded room, examining Akeila. When she received her diploma and smiled, his heart skipped a beat because he felt as though she was smiling for him. She was beautiful, and her smile still lit up rooms. Her long, curly hair was falling over her shoulders, and the cap sat neatly on her head. Her face was lightly made up, and when she smiled, her lips shone, exposing white teeth. He heard the guy sitting next to him whispering how gorgeous she was, and a bolt of jealousy filled his heart. She looked so young, happy, and radiant, and he could not take his eyes of her. He could not see who she was looking at in the front of the room, but he assumed that it was her family. The family shared a bond, and he knew that they would never miss out on such a special landmark in her life. Did she even think about him? She seemed to be doing quite well without him, and it hurt. His anger intensified as the ceremony came to an end.

Akeila said good-bye to some of her classmates and then joined her family, who was waiting for her. Everyone wanted to leave at the same time, making it very difficult for her to get to them even though they were not very far away. She stood immobile, waiting for the crowed to subside, and then she saw a familiar face walking toward her. She blinked and then gently rubbed her eyes, hoping that the image would go away. Was her mind playing games with her? Her secret wish was that her husband would be here to celebrate with her, but she knew that was impossible. She stood in her tracks motionless as the image drew closer. It became clearer and more real, and her heartbeat increase.

"Hello, Akeila. You look like you have seen a ghost," Che' whispered, looking at her with a mysterious gleam in his eyes. When she remained speechless with her mouth slightly opened, he added, "Would you like to pinch me, to ensure that I am real?"

"Hello, Che'. Is it really you?" she asked, incredulous. She slowly walked into his arms and then wrapped her own around his waist as tears threatened to fall.

Che' was shocked by her reaction at seeing him. On impulse he slowly hugged her. She felt so good in his arms that he did not want to let her go.

"What are you doing here?" she asked, gently pulling herself from his arms as she regained her composure.

"I have come to see you graduate," he said sarcastically while looking at her square in the eyes.

Akeila knew that something was wrong because his eyes were cold and calculating. "How did you know about my graduation?" She quickly checked the area where her family was standing. The crowd was diminishing, and she did not want to deal with Che' in here.

"I am head of Homeland Security and am very good at it. Did you forget?" Che' answered, smiling as he continued to glare at her with serious eyes.

"I know that you are. However, why did you seek me out after four years?" Akeila queried. She sensed that he had a hidden agenda, and it frightened her. He was rich, ruthless, and powerful, and he had the resources to take away the most important thing in her life. She didn't want to deal with him right now, and she desperately wanted to get away from him. She needed some time to formulate a plan to protect her child.

"Is there somewhere that we can talk in private?" Che' asked in is a stern.

"Now is not a good time, Che'," she answered nervously, looking in the direction where her family was. They were busily chatting among themselves, but it was only a matter of time before they realized that she had company. The crowd was diminishing, and she wanted to be free of him before he and her family noticed each other. "Can I meet you somewhere tomorrow?"

Che' looked at Akeila and realized that she was nervous. The way that she kept looking at the crowd made him wonder who she was looking for. *Is it her lover?* he wondered as his anger surfaced. "Tomorrow? After stealing from me and betraying me, don't you think that you owe me a few minutes of your precious time?" he said vehemently, and anger grew in his black eyes.

"What are you . . . ?"

Before Akeila could finish her sentence, Che' grabbed her forcefully by the arm and led her toward the exit. "You are coming with me right now, whether you like it or not," he ordered quietly.

Akeila realized that he was beyond rational thinking. It terrified her even more.

"Leave my mommy alone!" Che' and Akeila were so engross in what they doing that they did not notice the upset toddler pulling on his shirt. "Leave my mommy alone!" Link screamed again as Che' set Akeila free in disbelief.

"Link, I am okay," Akeila said quietly, quickly taking her son in her arms as the family gathered around with confused looks.

Che' stood there speechless, staring at the little boy in Akeila's arms. It was as though he was looking at a picture of himself when he was that age. *God, could that be my son?* he thought, and his heart started beating very quickly. Thoughts of him going into cardiac arrest crossed his mind as his breathing quickened. A feeling of weakness overpowered him, and he was going to pass out.

"Che', are you okay?" Akeila asked, quickly taking hold of his arm and leading him to a chair.

His eyes remained fixed on Link, who followed close behind her. "Is he my son, Akeila?" he asked, grabbing hold of her arm. "Tell me, is he my son?"

"We will discuss this later," she answered quietly, looking pleadingly at her son. When Che' took his eyes away from the kid, the Morrow family was standing around him with anger and resentment blazing in their eyes. He knew that his emotion needed to be under control in order to deal with this situation.

"Mommy, why was this man hurting you?" Link asked as he held onto her hand protectively.

"He was not hurting me, honey. He is my friend and only wanted to speak to me," she whispered quietly, caressing his cheeks. She then looked at Che', and her heart reached out to him. He sat there quietly with a million questions in his eyes as he looked at her for answers. "Che', this is my son, Link."

"Nice to meet you, Link," Che' said, mustering up all the strength that he had at the moment. He hugged the toddler while tears threatened to fall from his eyes.

The Morrow family looked at father and son embracing each other for the first time. It was very moving, like a scene from a movie, and they were speechless.

"Mommy, your friend hugged me tight," Link said, smiling as he went to his mom, who stood by quietly.

"Mom and Dad, could you please take Link to the car? We will be there shortly," Pam said, breaking the silence. Most of the people had left, and she knew that Akeila needed to get over the shock of seeing Che'.

"What the hell are you doing here, Che'?" Tasha asked, glaring at him angrily. "Why did you have to come and ruin Akeila's special day?"

Che' was not in the frame of mind to deal with Akeila's sisters. All he wanted right now was to have his questions answered. Presently he knew that this was impossible because of the closeness of the Morrow family. He may as well answer their questions if he wanted them to be civil toward him.

"I came to see your sister graduate," he said with confidence, getting a grip on his emotions.

"Oh please. Do you expect us to believe that?" Pam answered furiously. "That's bull, and you know it."

"Why are you being so concerned all of a sudden?" Tasha said, glaring at him.

Che' looked at the Morrow sisters as they scrutinized him and eagerly anticipated his answers. The three possessed some similar qualities, yet they could not be more different. They were very gorgeous and had the same round face, warm personalities, and great intelligence. However, the similarities ended there. Pam was overprotective and very structured, Tasha was wild and spontaneous, and Akeila was a bit of both. His eyes focused on Akeila, who stood there quietly with questions in her big, brown eyes.

"I would like to talk to Akeila alone, please," he requested softly.

"You will talk to her, but first you need to tell us why you are here," Pam replied, still glaring at him. "Are you here to hurt my sister?"

Che' remained quiet, knowing that she was right. That was his main intention, but after seeing Link, he was confused and had no idea as to his course of actions.

"Just what we thought," Tasha said. "You may be powerful, but it you believe that we are going to step aside and allow you to cause Akeila any more pain, you are greatly mistaken."

"What are you talking about?" Che' asked with a confused look on his face. "I have never done anything to offend your sister."

"Oh please, aren't you the guy who married my sister, took her to a strange country, and then turned around and cheated on her? To top it off, you allowed your mother to verbally abuse her!" Pam concluded breathlessly. "I hate you, Che' Athien, for what you did to her."

"What the hell are you babbling about?" Che' said in disbelief as he looked at Akeila, who remained indecipherable. "I did no such thing."

"Listen, guys, here is not the place for this," Tasha said slowly, observing the few people who were starting to stare at them.

"I do not care about that," Che' said angrily. "You cannot accuse me of such hideous crimes and not expect me to defend myself."

"There is no defense possible that can take away the pain that you have caused my sister," Pam replied. "But Tasha is right—not here. We are going to dinner to celebrate our sister's accomplishment, and you can join us if you like."

"Are you crazy, Pam?" Tasha said in astonishment.

"Only if Akeila say that it's okay. They have to talk," Pam said.

The three looked at Akeila, who had remained inaudible through this whole ordeal. There were so many questions in her mind that only Che' could answer. "Yes, he can come," she replied quietly. "We are going to talk afterward."

"Just remember, Akeila, you do not owe him anything, not even an explanation," Tasha added, and she rushed out of the room.

"Come here, Akeila," Pam said, putting her arms protectively around her sister. She knew that this was not a tranquil experience in seeing her husband and him meeting their son for the first time. "The family is waiting. Let's go." They walked toward the exit.

On the way to the restaurant, the Morrow family busily conversed among themselves as they try to figure out Che's reason for coming. Akeila sat silently in the limousine with her son nearby. There were a million questions flooding her mind, but the one that was precedence was that of her son. Had Che' found out about Link and wanted to take him away from her? Although he seemed very surprised to see him, she knew that he had the resources and could definitely do so. On impulse she quickly wrapped her arms around Link and then gently ruffled his curly hair as he smiled at her. He was her life, and no one was ever going to take him away from her.

Che' drove slowly behind them, not knowing or caring where he was going. The green trees and bushes by the roadside were not quite visible to him, either. Even though there was a refreshing breeze blowing in the atmosphere, he could not feel it. Questions kept popping up in his mind. *Is Link really my son? Why does the family believe such bad things about me?* he wondered. He needed answers and was definitely going to get them.

The dinner was eaten in near silence, with Link the only person making conservation. He was a diversion that everyone was happy to capitalize on. After the quick dinner, the family reluctantly departed, giving Akeila and Che' the privacy that they needed.

It was around nine thirty, and the Manhattan restaurant was starting to get very busy and crowded. The area was divided into two sections: private booths where they were, and open sitting. The lights were dim and the soft music gave the place a very romantic feeling. Most of the people dining were couples who were greatly engrossed in each other. The waiters and waitresses were impressively dressed and did their jobs with skill and grace. Che' and Akeila scrutinized each other with great intensity; neither knew how to start the conversation where there were so many unanswered questions.

Che' quickly ordered a shot of whisky, and as soon as the waiter served him, he addressed Akeila. "Why the hell didn't you let me know that I had a son?" he blurted out, angrily drinking down a shot of whisky. "He *is* my son, right?"

"Of course he is your son," Akeila replied, stunned by his question. "He looks just like you."

"Then why did you keep him away from me? Do you hate me that much?" he asked, taking another shot while searching her eyes for answers. "You know how much I wanted to have a family."

Akeila looked at Che' and recognized that he was in a lot of emotional pain after finding out that Link was his son and he was never a part of his son's life. However, Che' was the reason why she had to leave, and her impiety slowly disappeared as she stated her case. "I am sorry that you had to find out this way, but I thought that you did not care," she said quietly.

"What do you mean, I don't care? You know how much I wanted to have children."

"You had a very strange way in showing that your family was the most important thing in your life," Akeila said angrily, remembering him kissing Michelle.

"I miss almost four years of my son's life," Che' said as he sat there unmoving, his broad shoulders rigid. "If you had come to me, I would have taken care of you both. Thinking that I do not care is not a good enough reason for keeping my son away from me."

"Oh really? Why don't you stop pretending to be the innocent victim!" Akeila screamed while fighting back angry tears as thoughts of his betrayal crowded her mind. The pain stills hurt as if it had happened yesterday.

"Crying? Is the best that you can do?" he said sarcastically, obviously not moved by her outburst. She remained silent and slowly took a drink of her water. "Aren't you going to tell me the truth?" he said furiously as thoughts of another man raising his son came to his mind.

"I *am* telling you the truth," Akeila said as her anger started to surge. "When I found out about the pregnancy, the first thing that I wanted to do was share the joyful news with you, so I came to your job to surprise you."

"You came to my job?" Che' repeated, looking curiously at her. She looked sad, and he could not understand why.

"That was my first time, and the staff was very pleasant to me, especially after I presented my ID and they realized that I was your wife. When I got to your office, guess what I saw." She said, glaring at him.

"I do not—"

"Michelle in your arms, and you, Che' Athien, kissing her!" she yelled before he could finish. Tears fell from her eyes.

Che' was very shocked by Akeila's explanation, so he remained speechless and stared at her. He knew that she did not make up that story. He remembered clearly that day Michelle came into his office, trying to convince him that they belonged together. "Akeila, please don't cry," he whispered softly when he saw the tears rolling down her face, and sadness rose in his heart. He imagined how shocked and brokenhearted she felt, and he wanted to comfort her. "I was never unfaithful to you when we were together," he said while reaching into his pocket to retrieve a handkerchief and gently dry her tears. "That day in my office was just a big misunderstanding."

"I know what I saw, Che," Akeila replied softly. "I have lived with that image in my mind for the past four years, so please do not try to make me doubt myself."

"Akeila, Michelle came into my office trying to persuade me to leave you, and when she recognized that wasn't going to happen, she then surprised me by sitting in my lap and kissing me unexpectedly," he explained. "I guess that's when you saw us. I was surprised and shocked at first because I thought that she had accepted our marriage."

Akeila remained quiet as she thought about the incident. Was he right? Did she misconstrue the situation?

"If you had stayed a little longer, you would have seen me ordering her out of my office," Che' added as he tried to convince her. He could see that the seed of doubt still existed in her eyes, and he wanted desperately for her to believe him.

Akeila gazed deeply into her husband's black eyes and realized that he was telling the truth. However, she did not feel blissful about it. Every decision that she had made for her future was based on that fact. She had suffered heartache and pain, thinking that he did not love her. Sweet music was playing in the background as couples danced on the dance floor. She took another sip of water and focused her attention on him again.

"Did you want to stay married to me?" Che' asked bluntly, drinking the last of his whiskey. None of his plan was going the way that he'd predicted. He was now drowning in the sea of the unexpected.

"Of course—I wanted this marriage," she replied. "You knew how much I loved you."

"I thought that you had loved me, but I was so wrong," he answered, watching her with eyes that she could not read.

"How could you say that, after what I have just shared with you?" Akeila probed, not understanding his motive for those questions.

"The moment you thought that I was unfaithful, you ran off with your lover, stealing a million pounds from me," he accused, never taking his eyes from her.

"Are you crazy?" she shouted, grabbing her purse and getting to her feet. She needed to get away so that she could get herself together.

"Oh no, we are going to finished this conservation," Che' said as he stood up and quickly grabbed her by the hand. "I have waited four years for that answer, so sit down."

Akeila sat down quickly, wishing that she had a shot of whiskey in front of her. She was not a big drinker, but the events leading up to when Che' reappeared in her life was too much for her to deal with at this moment. Even though she was not surprised by his accusation, she was a little stunned by the events leading up to it. His mom and Michelle were a very devious team, and she knew that he'd had no choice but to believe their lies.

"Who was he?"

"There was no one, Che'," Akeila whispered. She did not know when all the anger that she'd felt a few minutes ago had disappeared. She felt very weak and was tired of hiding her true feelings. She missed her husband and still loved him. She did not want to fight or be strong anymore. "From the moment that I met you, there has been no one else, and when I married you, I was always true to my vows. I loved you with my whole heart, and there is no room for another," she concluded, taking his hand.

Che' closed his fingers around her small hand; it felt so good touching her. He looked into her brown eyes and was convinced that she was telling the truth, which made him feel relieved. Revenge and divorce ceased to exist in his mind as he tried to understand.

Akeila said, "I never stole from you."

"Please explain, because the money is gone."

"After I left your office, I went to the estate, and your mom found me crying," Akeila said. "I felt hurt and helpless, and I explained the situation to her. To my surprise she was happy to inform me that you only pitied me and had never loved me. She pointed out that Michelle was the future of the Athien family and asked me how much it would take for me to disappear from your life."

"Akeila, I am so sorry," Che' murmured when he saw tears falling from her eyes.

"I thought that I had lost you. I was pregnant and needed the money, so I took it to start over," she sobbed. He wanted to comfort and ease her pain as she recalled that painful moment. On impulse he got up and slowly took her in his arms, and she cried away the pain.

"Come, Akeila, we will finish this conservation in the car," he said, leading her out of the restaurant under the gaze of curious eyes. When they got into the car, he took his handkerchief and dried her eyes and face while she remained motionless, looking into his eyes.

"I knew that I had to take care of the baby, so I took the money. Afterward she made me write that hateful note," Akeila added, crying some more.

"That was very wise of you in thinking about the future in such a sad situation. Don't worry about the money, because it was used to take care of you and my son."

Che' hated seeing his wife hurt and distorted; she looked so small and vulnerable. Her bright eyes were now red, and her face was stained with mascara. He had spent the past four years trying to hate her, but the fact was that they had been separated by malicious lies and vindictive people. "Oh Akeila," he whispered, taking her in his arms and trying to erase her pain. They held each other tightly, drawing strength from one another. "I am so sorry that you had to go through all that." Then he lightly touched her lips with his. He backed away a few inches and looked into her eyes. Her chin trembled while her bottom lip quivered. She then parted her lips as his mouth descended upon hers with great urgency. His tongue slipped in and stroked hers, seeking a deeper union, and she held him tightly around his neck. He could not stop himself from kissing her, and when her soft lips responded to his kisses, he explored her mouth some more.

Akeila clung to his broad shoulders while he held her head in place with one hand and used the other to caress her lower back. She moaned as his mouth left hers and then traveled along her neck, kissing lightly. He slowly unbuttoned her shirt, and his fingers found her breast, caressing lightly. She moaned softly, tilting her head backward as it rested on the leather seat. Che' replaced his hand with his mouth, and when he sucked her small, round breast, she shivered.

"Che'," Akeila moaned, knowing that she wanted so desperately to be with him. This change of events was happing so quickly, and she welcomed it.

"What, darling? Do you want me to stop?" he asked, lifting his head and looking at her with curious eyes.

"No," Akeila said, smiling, "but making love in the front seat of a car is very uncomfortable."

"Oh. Let's get out of here, then," Che' said, laughing.

CHAPTER 4

The room at the hotel was elegant and very beautiful; however, Akeila did not have the inquisitiveness to observe it. Her mind was on her husband and how much she wanted to make love to him. Since leaving him, she had not been intimate with anyone, so her body was now craving his touch. Che' held her hand as he led her to the huge bed. He took her face in his hand and studied it for a few seconds while she gazed at him with desire in her eyes. Then he lowered his head and kissed her softly. With hurried fingers he removed her clothes and then held her tightly, loving the feel of her naked body against his.

"I want you, Akeila," he said hoarsely, trying to control his need for her.

"I want you too, Che'," she answered, and with trembling fingers she started to undress him. He quickly shed the rest of his clothes and then lifted and put her on the bed. He caressed her neck as he put her nipples in his mouth and sucked. Akeila caressed his back as he lowered his mouth to her navel and then let it travel to her most intimate area; she moaned in pleasure. Che' was big, hard, and aroused as he pleasured her. She understood his hunger because she felt it too. He lowered his body enough to brace himself on his elbow and kiss her passionately. He kissed and caressed her all over her body, from her lips to her toes and her most intimate spot.

"Che'," she moaned as his lips, tongue, and teeth replaced his fingers. He knew exactly how to please her. Her nipples stood rigid as he nibbled and sucked on them. "Che', I want you inside of me," Akeila moaned, not able to endure anymore. She opened her legs, inviting him in.

"Not yet, baby," he whispered with passion in his voice. Aching with the need to have him inside her, Akeila grasped his buttocks and pulled him. He slid between her legs, caressing her famine core before she could pull him into her. His tongue replaced his finger, and with his head between her legs, he sucked.

"Che'!" she screamed breathlessly.

He then realized that she was wet and shivering and could not speak anymore. Her eyes rolled back as he loved her with his mouth and fingers all over again. As the tension built up, she climaxed multiple times. With aftershocks tingling in and around her feminine core, he lifted her hips and plummeted into her as she screamed. He loved how she felt, her taste, her smell, and her moaning as he rode her. She grabbed his waist and matched his rhythm. She screamed, and he grunted like a wild animal as they reached the peak of their passion.

Moments later in the aftermath of their lovemaking, Akeila lied in his arms, and Che' said softly, "Tell me about our son."

"When he was born, he weighed six pounds nine ounces and did everything ahead of schedule; he even walked at nine months," Akeila said, smiling as she thought about Link.

"Was it a difficult birth?"

"Yes, it was. I was in labor for twenty-four hours before Link decided to grace the world with his presence," Akeila replied, laughing.

"I am so sorry that you had to do this alone," Che' whispered softly, regretting how much he had missed out in his son's life.

"I was not alone. Pam and Tasha stayed with me in the delivery room, and my parents were outside. My sisters never left me, not until Link was born," she said proudly. "They took turns staying with him until he was two years old. It was mainly my mom and dad, but my sisters came when they got vacation time from their jobs. They did not want him to go to a day care so young because I was going to school full-time and working."

"You've got a remarkable family," Che' said, smiling when he learned that she was not alone. From the first moment that he'd met the Morrow family, he knew that they were unique. Anyone who was around them could feel the love and respect that they had for each other. Sometimes he envied the loyalty and commitment that they had for each other. As an only child, his parents loved him dearly, but while growing up he was always surrounded by nannies and hired help; he missed the family relationship. He desperately wanted to be there for his wife but was very relieved that she was with the people that loved her.

"Speaking of family," Akeila said, looking at the clock and then jumping from the comfort of her husband arms. "I'd better be on my way." She began getting dressed quickly.

"Yes, I know. They are probably wondering what happened to you," Che' said sadly, missing her already. "After all, they think that I am a horrible person." He got up from the bed and slowly pulled on his pants.

"Che', we are going to straighten this whole thing out," she said while looking at his sad face, and then she smiled. All she wanted to do was to remain in his arms and be loved. "You can get to know your son—after all, it is not right for me to keep Samos Athien away from his father."

"Oh my God, Akeila, you named him after my father?" he shouted in disbelief, grabbing and lifting her up in his arms.

"I knew that would make you happy," Akeila said, laughing as she put her arms around his neck.

Having her in his arms felt right, and so he took that opportunity to kiss her neck and then slide her slowly against his half naked body, not letting her feet touch the ground. He realized that he was aroused, and his mouth took possession of hers.

"Che'," she murmured breathlessly, "I have to go."

"I know, baby."

"Then put me down," she said, but she remained in his arms as he kissed her deeply. He used one hand to lift her skirt up and then gently push his finger inside her. Realizing that she was wet, he unbuttoned his pants while still kissing her. Then he lifted her onto his erection as he slowly slid into her. She breathed quickly and wrapped her legs tightly against his waist, her arms going around his neck as he plunged into her over and over.

"God, Akeila," Che' groaned after spilling his seeds inside her. The need to exercise more self-control was something that he had to do, but she felt good, which made him weak. He withdrew and then placed her gently on the ground. Moments later Che' whispered, "Let me take you home." With sadness in his heart, he held out his hand to her, and she quietly took hold of it.

"Mommy, Mommy, wake up!" Link shouted, shaking her.

"What, baby?" Akeila said lazily as she sat up, rubbed her eyes, and then looked at her son with a smile. He was wearing a pair of blue Lightning McQueen pajamas and cotton slippers on his feet. "It's only seven o'clock, honey. I can sleep a little longer."

"No it's not, Mommy. Aunty Tasha said that it is twelve o'clock," Link answered.

"Oh my!" she said quickly, looking at the clock on her dressing table. She did not realize that it was so late. She reached out, playfully grabbed her son, and tickled him as he rolled all over the bed.

"Stop, Mommy!" Link said, laughing hysterically.

"I am going to eat you for breakfast," she teased as he giggled.

"Aunty Pam made breakfast already." Link laughed as his mom nibbled on his ears. "Mommy, she throws up lots."

"Is she okay, baby?" Akeila asked, jumping out of bed and taking Link in her arms as she rushed to the leaving room.

45

Pam lay on the couch with her eyes closed. She look pale and helpless, and Akeila's heart reached out to her. She had never seen her sister look that way before; she was always lively and in control. Even though Pam's favorite soap opera *General Hospital* was in progress, she was not aware of it. Akeila placed Link on the couch next to his aunt and then gently reached out and held her hand. Pam slowly opened her eyes.

"Are you okay, Pam?" she asked with a worried look. Her sister was her rock, and now she did not know how to help her.

"Stop looking at me like you think that I am going to die," Pam said weakly. "I feel faint and light-headed. Everything that I eat, I throw up."

"That is a possibility that you may have caught a virus," Akeila noted. "It happens sometimes when you travel from different regions."

"Maybe I did."

"Where is everyone?" Akeila asked, looking around in disbelief. It seems odd that the rest of her family would leave Pam sick all by herself. She went to the refrigerator, took a glass of ginger ale, and handed it to her sister.

"Mommy, can I have some juice, please?" Link interrupted as he drove his toy plan all over the leaving room area.

"Sure, baby, here it is." She handed it to him, and he walked away to watch television in the next room.

"Tasha went to the pharmacy to get me some medication, and Mom and Dad went to do some last-minute shopping, seeing that we are going home tomorrow," Pam answered as she took small sips of the drink. "Your brother-in-law is very worried. He is in Germany right now but called over twenty times this morning."

Akeila smiled when she thought about Roger. He was a very devoted husband to her sister, and even though the couple spent a lot of time apart, they always found time for each other. He bought all the latest gadgets so that they could communicate as much as possible. "I bet he is worried, but you will be fine."

"He told me that he is going to take two weeks off work so that he can take care of me." Pam blushed as she looked at her sister, who looked radiant and happy.

"That sounds great," Akeila said, smiling as she thought of Che' and how much she missed him.

"Akeila, what happened between you and Che' last night?" Pam asked. "You came home very late."

"I would also like to know the answer to that question," Tasha said as she walked into the room with a bag in her hand.

"Let's take care of our sister first, and then I will answer all your questions," Akeila said, blushing while her sisters looked at each other.

"Where is the medication?" Pam asked, sitting up.

"Here it is," Tasha answered, handing her a pregnancy test.

"What are you . . . ?" Akeila said in shock.

"Wait, Akeila, let her take the test," Tasha replied. "After talking to the doctor at the pharmacy, he told me that her symptoms indicated that she may be pregnant."

"Why are you doing this?" Pam whispered, and then she started crying. "You know that I cannot conceive. I have been trying for the past eight years with no success."

"Pam, remember the doctor said that there is nothing wrong? You and Roger are young and in perfect health," Akeila said quietly, and then she hugged her sister. "Maybe now is your time."

"Pam, I am so tired of seeing you stress over not getting pregnant," Tasha said slowly. "Have you ever considered the possibility that because of Roger's job schedule, whenever he is home and you two make love, you may not be ovulating?" Pam and Akeila looked at each other and then at Tasha. What she said made perfect sense. There were only a few days in a woman cycle when she could get pregnant. "Why are you two looking at me like that?" Tasha said with a big grin on her face. "I do have a college education, and even though you two forget it at times, we Morrow women are very educated."

"Take the test," Akeila said softly as Tasha handed it to Pam. "What do you have to lose?"

"Okay, I will," Pam said, and then she hesitantly took it and headed to the bathroom.

Both sisters waited patiently for Pam, who emerged from the bathroom minutes later, holding the test in her hand. They looked at the clock and the result window, waiting anxiously for an answer. When a positive showed up, the sisters started screaming happily and then started to cry. Hours later they came from the doctor's office with Pam carrying a sonogram picture of her eighteen-week-old baby.

Che' quickly got out of the shower and slowly began making preparations to meet his in-laws. Akeila had called minutes ago, inviting him over to dinner. He had done the routine many times in the past, but presently he felt very nervous. Proving to them that he was not a part of the conspiracy to make his wife disappear was something that he desperately wanted to do. His wife . . . just thinking about her brought a smile to his face. After dropping her off late last night, he came back to his hotel room and let thoughts of her consume him. He saw in his mind's eye ways to make up for all the pain that she had been through. He had not felt so happy and contented in years—in fact, not since she had left him. When he left England, never in his wildest dreams did he imagine that they would come together like this. All he'd wanted were answers and revenge, but instead he found ecstasy. She was the only woman who could satisfy his body and soul. He loved her touch, smell, and the feel of her body close to his, and the way that she moaned and screamed his name. Her big, brown eyes would grow weak in fulfillment after they made love. He loved her body, which had not changed much; she was just a little curvier, and he believed that it was because of the birth of their son.

Che' had a son who was named after his dad, whom he love and miss dearly. His father was a great husband and dad, and he knew that his presence was significantly missed on the estate. Akeila honored him greatly by giving their son his name, even though she believed that Che' was unfaithful. That spoke volumes as to the type of person that she was, and he silently vowed that he would love her forever. He had spent the day making plans for their future and knew that he wanted his family back. He called his job and extended his vacation time, which was not difficult because he had not taken a vacation in four years. Spending as much time as possible with them was the first step in accomplishing his goal. After talking to his lawyers, he then had a very lengthy discussion with his contractor. He believed that God had given him a second chance, and he was definitely going to do things right this time. He knew that Akeila still had feelings for him by the way that she gave her body completely when they made love, and that was good enough for now.

Che' looked at his reflection in the mirror and was very satisfied with what he saw. He was casually dressed in a white short-sleeve shirt that made his muscular shoulders quite visible, as well as black slim jeans and black Prada dress shoes. As he was about to leave, he heard a beep on his cell phone and thought that it was Akeila; they have been texting regularly during the day. He was greatly disappointed when he realized that it was Michelle stating that she missed him and that he should called his mom. He still couldn't fathom the way that his mom treated Akeila, and he wondered why she'd conspired with Michelle to destroy the most important thing in his life. She would definitely have some explaining to do. As for Michelle, it was over. Right now he did not want to think about those women; when he got back to England, he would deal with them accordingly. He took one last look at himself and was on his way.

The Morrows spent the afternoon cooking and making all the necessary preparations for dinner. It was a beautiful summer evening, and everyone was in a good mood. The atmosphere in the cozy apartment was that of laughter and joy. Akeila sat on the couch as she waited anxiously for Che' to arrive. After the night that they'd spent together, she could not stop thinking about him and missed him terribly. The knowledge that he did not betray her made it easier to trust in her heart, which was always filled with love for him. She looked at her son, who was playing a blocks game with Pam, and she knew that this was going to be a very special moment for him and his dad. After informing the family that Che' was not unfaithful, they were relieved but were still upset with him. She hoped that this dinner would be a new beginning for the people that she loved. When the doorbell rang, she rushed to the door while she announced Che' arrival.

"Good evening," she whispered shyly.

"Good afternoon, Akeila," Che' greeted, smiling as he looked her over. She was wearing a mini denim skirt that showed off her smooth and toned legs, a flowered silk blouse, and black high heel wedges. Her long hair fell luxuriously over her shoulders. "You look beautiful."

"Thank you," she replied with a smile that took his breath away. "And you look very handsome."

Che' smiled and took Akeila's hand as they walked into the room. The touch of her fingers against his made him want to take her into the bedroom and ravish her; however, he knew that this behavior was inappropriate with her family here.

"Good afternoon, Mr. And Mrs. Morrow. Good afternoon, Pam and Tasha," he greeted politely, not knowing if he should hug them or shake their hands as they walked into the room. Then he let his attention focus on his son, who stood looking at him with curious eyes.

"Mommy, why is your friend here?" Link asked, walking up to his mother and holding on to her hand very protectively.

"He is joining us for dinner and wants to spend some time with you," Akeila said, leading Che' to the couch.

"Why, Mommy? Does he want to be my friend too?" Link asked, looking at Che' and smiling.

Akeila realized that the time was here for her to tell her son about his dad, who stood there smiling back at him. "Honey, remember I have told you that your daddy was living in a faraway country? Well, Che' is your daddy, and he is here to see you."

"Really, Mommy? I have a daddy!" he shouted happily, jumping into father's arms.

Che' held the tiny body close to his heart, and he would cherish this moment forever as he fought back tears that were threatening to fall. "I am your daddy, Link, and I am so happy to meet you," he said, kissing him all over while the family looked on.

"Daddy, do you want to play a block game with me?" Link said as he led his father away happily.

The family had a very enjoyable dinner, and shortly afterward Akeila carried a tired Link to bed. Che' took that opportunity to notice his surroundings. The apartment was very clean and homely. Pictures of the family were posted on the walls, and one when Link was a newborn caught his eyes. It was precious and priceless, and a sad feeling came upon him for a quick moment. He then came to his senses under the piercing eyes of his in-laws, who were focused on him. He knew that it was only a matter of time before they confronted him. He was very grateful for the way that they had made him feel welcome and include in him the evening activities.

"I would like to apologize to you all for hurting Akeila, and most important for the role that my mother played in making her unhappy," he said, looking from one family member to the next. "I take full responsibility for not protecting her or being there for her, especially at a time when she needed me most. I should not have left it up to my mother to take care of my responsibility." He then looked at Akeila, who walked slowly over to him and sat down.

"We understand how important your job is," Mr. Morrow said. "But you have to remember that my daughter was a stranger to your country, your culture, and your family."

"You are right. I should have been more considerate and thoughtful of what she was going through," Che' said with regret.

"Che' trusted his mother to be there for Akeila in his absence, and that was his biggest mistake," Tasha stated.

"I really trusted her with my wife's happiness—after all, she is my mom," Che' said as he looked at Akeila, who sat quietly at his side.

"Marriage is not easy, but the key to it is communication and honesty," Mrs. Morrow stated. She and her husband had been married for fifty years and were still very much in love. "And you two fail miserably at it."

"The fact is that Che's mom is a very evil woman," Pam said angrily, looking at her brother-in-law. When he remained quiet and did not even trying to defend his mom, she continued. "Do you know all the despicable things that they did and said to my sister?"

"Pam, that's the past," Akeila interrupted quietly as she tried to put that period of her life behind her.

"He should know, sister shrink," Pam replied, "Then you can finally put all this behind you and move on with your life."

"What did they do?" Che' asked, curiously looking at Akeila.

When she did not answer, Pam continued, "She was called a gold digger and a third-world tramp. What's more it was in the presence of other people, and thy even laughed at her. My sister was prevented from venturing into certain parts of the house and had to eat most of her meals in her room because she was scared of running into your mother."

"Oh my God, Akeila! I did not know all this was going on," Che' murmured, shocked by his mother's actions. "Why didn't you say something?" He reached out and took her hand, wanting to give her comfort and even protect her from the incidents that had happened five years ago.

"I did not want to bother you with my problems. After all, you were working hard on that new job and trying to prove yourself."

"What my mother and Michelle did to you was cruel and abusive," he said angrily. "Under no circumstance would I have tolerated this kind of behavior."

"Your job—"

"I know how important my job is, Akeila," he interrupted furiously. "But don't you know that your happiness was the top priority to me? You really had me fooled in believing that you were happy."

"I was happy with you, Che'," she said softly. She looked pleadingly into his eyes so that he could understand.

Nothing else seemed to exist as he reached out and took her in his arms. "Baby, you did not trust in the love that we have and the vows that we took," he said softly. "You should have trusted in that, and things would have turned out differently."

"I am so sorry," Akeila cried as the tears fell from her eyes. Che' was right: if she'd had faith in him, his mother and Michelle would not have the ammunition that they had in order to destroy their marriage. She sobbed as he held her tightly, comforting her.

"Che', I believe that your mother brainwashed Akeila into believing that you would not choose her over your mother," Tasha stated quietly.

"That would have never happened," he whispered, smiling reassuringly at Akeila as he dried the tears from her eyes. "It took me such a long time to find you, and I will always put you first."

The Morrow family looked at Che' and Akeila and saw the extraordinary love that they shared. They realized that even though the couple had gone through so much and had been separated, their love had remained solid.

"Why didn't you all tell me what was going on when I came to Grenada, looking for Akeila?" Che' asked as he observed his in-laws.

"You came to Grenada looking for me?" Akeila asked with a surprised look on her face, and then she glared at each family member. When they did not answer, it became obvious to her that they had known. "Why wasn't I told?"

"You needed time to concentrate on yourself and the pregnancy," Pam said softly. "Most important, you needed to accomplish some of your dreams without any obstacles or anyone standing in your way."

"I understand partly what you are saying, Pam," Che' said hoarsely. "But why did you lead me to believe that your sister never loved me? You even told me that the stolen money was payment for a miserable marriage and that she had found a better lover than me."

"Pam!" they all shouted together as they glared at her in surprise. Obviously the whole family was clueless about that conversation.

"Did you say all those hurtful things to him, honey?" Mrs. Morrow said with disappointment in her voice. "Don't you know that he would be devastated after hearing it?"

"Don't be mad at her. Pam only did what she thought was best in the situation," Tasha said, looking at Akeila, who quietly scrutinized her older sister.

"Akeila," Pam said softly, "when I listened to your cries, I felt your pain and wanted you to get out of this situation and reach your true potential. When you left Che', I knew that this was your chance to do so, and that's why I lied. You are my little sister, and I always want what's best for you. Look at you now—confident, strong, and with an occupation that you have always dreamed of."

Akeila walked over to her sister and hugged her tightly. She knew that Pam was right, and everyone understood why she'd said those words.

"Che' called me last week wanting to know how you were," Pam said. "I was very surprised, but I flaunted and boasted to him that you would be graduating from Hofstra University with your doctorate. Now, days later, here he is. I knew that he is intelligent and very good at his job, and that's why I had to lie."

"Is that how Che' found out where Akeila was?" Tasha asked, laughing and then playfully tapping him on his shoulders. "I was wondering how he found out. Damn, you are good."

"Che'," Pam said, smiling as she extended her hand, "please take good care of my sister. God knows that I will not have the time to do so myself, with a baby on the way."

Che' looked at his sister-in-law smiling at him with her hand extended in friendship, and he smiled himself. She was always polite to him but also very reserved. He gently took her hand and pulled her into his arms. The family laughed while they hugged and kissed each other. The cozy room was filled with forgiveness, compassion, love, and hope for the future. They talked for quite some time and then informed Che' that they would be leaving tomorrow to go back to Grenada.

Akeila looked at her family and was very impressed with the way that they had dealt with their problems. Everyone that she loved was happy and getting along, giving them reason to celebrate life. "Let me take you for a night out in the Big Apple, Che'," she said, grabbing his hand and pulling him playfully to the door.

CHAPTER 5

The Empire State Building is *the* location in New York City, and there is a very clear view of the city in all its splendor. The 102-story skyscraper, which is the tallest building in the city, was built in 1931 and has defined the New York skyline ever since. It's a great tourist destination and there is usually a crowd of people waiting to experience its magnificence.

Che' and Akeila did not have to wait in line because most of the visitors had already left. Afterward, they strolled through Rockefeller Center and Fifth Avenue, the fashion streets of the city, and did some eye shopping. Even though the stores were already close, there were a lot of people leisurely walking around and enjoying the view and the energy of the place. 'The city that never sleeps" was a very appropriate name for the place.

On the way home to Brooklyn, the couple stopped off at the Cornice Pear, which reminded them of the time when they first fell in love. This place was a favorite spot for families and loved ones to visit in the summer time. There were facilities made to accommodate barbecuing, fishing, and kite flying. The clear blue sky was filled with stars, and the moon shined in all its glory. The night was peaceful with the gentle splashing of the waves against the man-made walls, and the slow dancing of trees as the wind blew. It was around midnight, and so there were only a few people there, which gave the place a very private setting.

Che' sat on the boardwalk with Akeila in his lap while he lightly stroked her hair and they gazed at the sky. He was so ecstatic and contented with his life. Everything was perfect, and he wanted it to stay that way; however, being totally honest with Akeila was something that he knew had to be done, and in the process he hoped that she understood. He desired to put his family together and thus was not going to allow secrecy to prevent that from happening.

"Akeila, there is something that I need to talk to you about," he said softly. "I hope that you do understand."

Akeila looked up into her husband's eyes and knew that whatever he had to tell her was not good news. She'd connected with him physically and emotionally, and the bonding between father and son and the forgiveness her family had bestowed upon him was so amazing. All this gave her an insight into her future, which looked very promising. She was so happy and did not want anything to change those feelings of hope. "What is it?" she asked softly.

"When I came to find you, my main intention was to make you pay for breaking my heart and stealing from me, and to get a divorce," he said slowly.

"We already went through this, Che," Akeila replied, smiling stroking his face lovingly. "That is in the past now."

"Michelle and I got engaged about a year ago," he blurted out quickly.

"You did what?" she shouted in disbelief, jumping out of his lap. "So right now you are cheating on your fiancée with you wife?"

"Michelle thought that you and I were divorce—in fact, everyone does," Che' answered, looking at her face as the light in her eyes disappeared and was replaced with hurt.

"Well, you have found me," she added angrily. "Do you have the divorce papers? I can sign them now so that you can be on your merry way."

"Akeila, please," he said pleadingly, reaching out to take her hand.

She angrily brushed him off and put some space between them. "Why did you come into my son's life, knowing that you had no intention of staying?" she asked, shaking her head in disbelief and trying to fathom the reality of what she was just told. "And you made love to me!"

"Akeila, stop it," Che' begged, wishing that he could take her into his arms and comfort her. "Listen, honey, I thought that you had left me for another, and I tried to move on."

"With all the different women in the world, you picked *Michelle* to move on with!" Akeila yelled. She did not care for that woman, who had always been hateful and unpleasant, causing her marriage to fall apart.

"Michelle was familiar, and we've known each other for a very long time. We socialize in the same circles, and my mother instigated the engagement," he explained, hoping that she could understand his point of view.

"I bet she did," she said, turning her back to him to observe the water, which was very serene. There were a number of small fish swimming, and they shined beautifully as the moon reflected on them. Akeila did not appreciates the beauty because her mind was now occupied with the seed of doubt in her heart about Che' and Michelle. She knew very well the history that they shared. "Tell me, Che', during our marriage, every time we made love, were you wishing that you were with Michelle and not me?"

"That's enough, Akeila!" Che' said angrily. He knew that she was upset; however, doubting the love that they shared was wrong. When she remained quiet with her back still turned, he slowly walked over and hugged her from behind. Once she tried to pull away, he held her tighter. "When we were together, I was always faithful to you, and deep in your heart I believe that you know it. Michelle is not the only woman that I had used to try and forget you with, and I have failed miserably. You, my love, are the only woman who has my heart and soul." When she remained silent he slowly turned her around and whispered, "Look at me, honey."

Akeila slowly lifted her head, gazed into her husband's eyes, and was startled by what she saw. His unfathomable, dark eyes were now radiating and overflowing with love for her. Like a woman who had been hypnotized, she saw his soul, which made all her doubts and fears disappeared. He continued. "You are my wife, the mother of my child, and I have never stopped loving you. I love you, Akeila." He kissed her softly on her lips. Che' was aware of her failure to reply, but when she kissed him back passionately, he knew there was hope for their marriage, and that was good enough for now. He would now have to prove to her that she and their son meant everything to him. That would not be a very difficult task to accomplish.

Over the next few weeks, Che', Akeila, and Link were inseparable. They spent a few nights at the luxurious Surrey Hotel as a family because Che' wanted them to experience some of the wonderful services that the hotel had to offer. There they were pampered and waited upon, and afterward he moved into Akeila's apartment, which felt so right. Link was very happy with having both of his parents around, and that was the beginning of a wonderful relationship between father and son. They did everything together, going to the beaches and museums, and dining out at the best restaurants in the city. It was all the more exceptional because they did it as a family.

Akeila took some time off from her job as a counselor at a local clinic so that she could be with her family. Spending the rest of her life with Che' was what she longed for, but she was terrified to trust in that dream. When they made love, it was incredible, and every time was like a new experience. Afterward they would lie in each other's arms and talk for hours about everything except their future. She loved her husband wholeheartedly, and he was the best husband and father. Visualizing a future without him was something that she could not do.

"What do you mean, he did not call?" Mrs. Athien asked. She looked at the woman sitting next to her on the luxurious couch at her home. Everything was sparking clean and arranged neatly, and her companion fit perfectly into her surroundings.

"Che' has been gone for weeks and does not even have the audacity to call me or return any of my calls," Michelle stated angrily. She got up and began pacing the floor in her Michael Koss sandals. She was casually attired in a long tie-dyed dress, and her long blonde hair was covered with a wide summer hat. "He has not answered my e-mail and text messages, which I believe is very rude."

"He has not called me, either," Mrs. Athien noted softly, trying to calm her future daughter-in-law. She did not understand why her son was acting so mysterious. A wedding between Che' and Michelle was going to be the social event of the year, and then they would give her the grandchildren that she desperately wanted. She would be the perfect wife for him because she came from a good English family, she was a social butterfly who knew how to entertain the wealthy, and she was very beautiful—these were characteristics that made her exceptional.

"Is that supposed to make me feel better?" Michelle said rudely. Then she took out her phone and dialed Che's number once more, and receiving his voicemail. "No answer! I cannot live like this, clueless to when I am going to get married. This is not good enough for me."

"Oh, I just remembered," Mrs. Athien answered, smiling affectionately. "I did speak to him a few weeks ago through his contractor."

"What do you mean?"

"My son is having some work done on the west wing and warned me to stay away from the premises," Mrs. Athien said, still livid with her son for treating her like an outsider. She had tried to sneak by to observe what was going on but was caught by his security guards, who then escorted her away. His cold words were, 'I am having some work done on the west wing, Mother, and I would appreciate it if you would stay away. If you don't, I have instructed security to make sure that you comply with my wishes."

"What kind of work, Mother?" Michelle inquired curiously as questions began to emerge in her mind.

"I do not know, seeing that I am not allowed to venture there," she replied, shaking her head. "My son has been behaving rather secretive."

"Something is definitely wrong," Michelle said, angrily grabbing her Gucci pocketbook from the couch. "I am going to get to the bottom of it."

"That's my girl," Mrs. Athien said, and then she kissed her future daughter-in-law good-bye.

Franko sat in his condo drinking a glass of chardonnay and smoking a Cuban cigar, which was his favorite thing to do for relaxation. There was a soccer game playing on the television, and England was in the lead, but that was not enough to keep his attention because his mind was consumed with thoughts of his revival. As the smoke from his cigar filled the room, the memories kept flooding his mind, and his anger resurfaced. *Che' Athien, the bastard! Where could he be?* he wondered. No one knew about Che's whereabouts. The only information that he received from his contacts was that Mr. Athien had left the country weeks ago on his private jet, destination unknown. Would Franko ever get his revenge? Four years had gone by, and his patience was running out. Giving up was not an option, but he was at that point where he wanted to do something drastic.

The ringing of the doorbell brought him back to reality. "Who the hell can this be," he said softly before walking toward the door and opening it. He was not surprised to see Michelle standing there. She had been sharing his bed for the past few weeks and was welcome at the condo at any time.

"I cannot believe that he left the country without telling me, and he has not called since!" she said, brushing past

Franko as he closed the door behind her. She flung her bag on the couch and then faced him with her fury.

"Who are you talking about, darling?" Franko asked, anxiously waiting for her answer because he knew that she was talking about her fiancé. He was her confidant, and he loved being that; when she had a problem, she would come for him to resolve it. She had become his most valuable informant, providing him with information about Che' that only someone close to him could obtain. Even though they were from different social classes, they had a lot in common: revenge, hate, and vengeance were some of the qualities that made their lovemaking electrifying.

"Che' left the country weeks ago, never bothering to call or get in touch with me," she stated indignantly. "I do not have any idea where he might be."

"Did you call his office?" he probed, trying to get as much information as possible.

"Of course I did, and his secretary treated me like a common stranger even though she knows who I am!" she yelled, taking a seat on the day bed that was present in the room.

"Easy, darling," Franko said gently as he walked up to her and began massaging her tense shoulders. "I can recall you saying that this guy has a very secretive job. Maybe he is on a case."

"You may be right, Franko, but I am scared because we had a very bad argument before he went away," Michelle replied, relaxing a little. "He is also doing some work on the estate, and no one except the workers is allowed to be there. Why is he being so secretive?"

"I do not know, but maybe he is trying to surprise you when he gets back," he answered convincingly.

"Do you really believe that?" Michelle asked smiling and wrapping her arms around his neck.

"No one can stay mad at you for long," Franko said, looking at her with passion in his eyes. "Tell me more about the estate."

"Why do you want to find out about the estate?" she questioned with a curious look.

"Well, it seems like a beautiful place," he said, cleverly kissing her long neck to distract her. "I would also like to visualize where my beautiful Michelle will be residing happily."

After talking about the estate for a few minutes, Michelle purred passionately, "Make love to me, Franko."

"My pleasure, baby," he whispered hoarsely, and with eagerly hands he hurriedly began taking of her clothes.

The August sun was beastly hot, and there was a heat advisory for New York City. Cooling centers appeared all around, and children could be seen playing in water from the fire hydrants. Everyone's main destination was the pool and beaches, where visiting time was extended for a few more hours. It was the worst time to be cooking, but Akeila was busy preparing dinner for her family. The air conditioner was running, but the kitchen felt like a furnace. They had been dining out frequently, so she wanted to make a home-cooked meal. On the menu was a green salad, steamed vegetables, steak, grilled chicken, macaroni and cheese, and a cheesecake for dessert. Knowing how much they love her cooking, she hurriedly set the table and placed the food on it. Che' and Link would be home at any moment; they had gone to the beach after unsuccessfully trying to convince her to accompany them. She quickly changed into a pair of Daisy Duke shorts and a white tank top, pulled her hair into a pony tail, and applied gloss to her lips.

When Che' entered the apartment, the aroma of food filled his nostrils. He had spent a wonderful time at the beach with his son; they had fun in the sun building sand castles and swimming in the cool, refreshing water. Although he was in good physical shape, being around a three-and-a-half-year-old boy sapped his energy. Still, he would not trade these moments for anything.

"Mommy, Mommy, where are you?" Link called out, rushing into the apartment.

"I am in the kitchen, honey," Akeila said, smiling as he ran into her waiting arms. "Did you have fun with Daddy?"

"Yes, I did! Daddy taught me how to swim," he said excitedly. "I made a sand castle too!"

"That's wonderful, Link," she said, looking at her husband as he entered the room. He was wearing a white V-neck T-shirt and cargo shorts. The summer sun had given him a natural, beautiful golden tan that highlighted his muscular physique and black eyes.

When Che' saw Akeila, he could not take his eyes of her. She was naturally beautiful. Her shorts showed off her toned legs, and her top clung tightly to her petite figure, exposing her round breasts, curves, and tiny waist. He wanted her so badly that he felt an urge in his groin even though he knew that he would have to wait to satisfy his sexual hunger.

"Time for both of you to wash up for dinner," she said, smiling shyly at Che' as he gazed at her with desire. Moments later they were all seated at the table, eating and conversing about the day's events. Che' bathed a tired Link and put him to bed afterward while Akeila tidied up the kitchen.

Che' walked toward his wife, who stood in front of the sink drying the last glass. When she put it into the cupboard, he slowly placed his hand around her waist, pulled her into him, and applied butterfly kisses on the back of her neck. Akeila tilted her neck sideways, giving him easy access to her neck, and she molded her body into him. He gently turned her into his arms, and his lips found hers in a soft, lingering kiss. When she responded passionately, he plunged his tongue into her mouth, seeking a deeper union while his tongue caressed hers, and then his hands found her breast. She moaned as his mouth traveled from her lips down to her neck and then sucked and nibbled on her breast. She wrapped her arms around his neck and pulled him close as her desire for him grew. He lifted her gently unto the sink as his tongue traveled to her belly button and then to her feminine core. She placed her legs around his neck, and he sucked, nibbled, and caresses her. Akeila cried out in pleasure when he pushed his finger into her.

"Oh Akeila," he groaned. She was so wet and ready for him. "I want you so bad, but not here." He lifted and then carried her in his arms to the bedroom. Che' laid Akeila on to the bed and slowly began taking of her clothes, never taking his eyes away from her. She lay naked and lovely, staring at him with love and passion in her brown eyes. He quickly got undressed and then scooped her up in his arms and took her to the shower. As the cool, refreshing water fell on their bodies, he hungrily kissed his wife, who clung to him and responded with hunger and desire. He took the body wash and sponge and then started washing her slowly and sensually as the water caressed her body. After gently pinning her hands over her head, up against the shower wall, he kissed her passionately. He was very aroused and hungry for her, and he slowly lifted her off her legs with his free hand and plunged into her as she screamed. He covered her mouth with kisses as he dove into her over and over again. She wrapped her legs around his waist and her arms around his neck, and she moved her waist to fit the rhythm that he created. They gloried in each other's bodies and cried out in sexual fulfillment.

Minutes later, they lay in each other's arms, very contented and satisfied. Che' knew that it was time for him to ask Akeila to go back to England with him tomorrow. He had received an urgent call from the English government stating that his services were needed. There was a group of terrorists who were a threat to the English subway. His private plane was fueled and ready to take off as soon as he ordered it. He had made all the necessary arrangements for his family to leave—without asking the most important person whose decision could alter the plans that he had made. What would he do if she said no? He could not and would not imagine a future without his family.

"Che', what's wrong?" Akeila asked, noticing his sadness. Knowing that something was wrong, she gently reached out and caressed his face, encouraging him to talk to her.

Che' looked into his wife's eyes and was more convinced that he could not live without her and his son. He knew that it would almost be impossible for him to relocate to New York, but if he had to do it in order for his family to stay together, he would. No sacrifice was too great for him to make for them.

"Baby, please talk to me," Akeila whispered softly.

"I have to fly back to England tomorrow, and I would like for you and Link to come with me," he said quickly before looking at her. She looked at him with a vague expression on her face and then rolled over and was about to get out of the bed. He grabbed her. "Oh no, we are going to talk about this," he murmured softly.

Akeila looked at Che' and knew that the moment had finally come for her to decide if she wanted to go back to England with him. She had been expecting it for quite some time and had already made her decision. She was petrified and nervous because she did not know how things would be this time around, and that created doubts in her mind. In her heart, however, she was convinced that the right decision was made, and she needed reassurance from him. "Would you put Link and I first at all times?" she asked, looking into eyes that could never lie to her. "And protect us always?"

"I promise you, Akeila Athien, that I will love, cherish, and protect you and our son, always," he whispered. Even though he did not say much, his eyes told her everything: the assurance of loyalty and everlasting love.

She said, "We will go with you to—"

Before Akeila could finish her sentence, Che' grabbed her and kissed her forcefully on the lips.

"Thank you, Akeila. I love you," he said, quite surprised that she had agreed to go with him so easily, especially given how painful her first experience was. He was expecting a struggle in convincing her but was proven wrong by the remarkable woman lying in his arms. Che' could not believe how blessed he was in finding her. She was so amazing, and as the day went by, his love for her grew deeper. He had left Woodstock a few months ago with pain and vengeance in his heart for the one person who had given him a family and unconditional love. He was thankful to God, faith, and destiny.

"Che', I love you too."

"Say it again."

"I love you, husband, now and forever."

"I will love you forever," Che' whispered softly as the kisses turned into a night filled with passion and ecstasy.

CHAPTER 6

"Mommy, Daddy, we are going to fly in a plane right now!" Link said excitedly while his father snapped on his seat belt.

"Yes, we are, honey," Akeila said, examining the private jet carefully. She knew that her husband was rich but never imagined the magnitude to which his wealth extended. There were several things about his life that were not known to her, but that was acceptable because she had a lifetime to find out. The interior of the luxury jet could have seated up to eight people. There were two decks; the top consisted of leather seats equipped with Internet access, cabin video screens, and music. She was amazed upon beholding the elegance of the lower dock. There was a cocktail bar that was fully stocked with a wide variety, a small dining area that seated up to four people, and a bedroom and shower. Everything was beautiful designed and arrange in a trendy style that took her breath away. The staff on board the flight consisted of a pilot and air hostess who had been employed with the family for a very long time.

It was a wonderful day to be flying: the winds were very calm, and the clear skies looked like a picture. After an hour into the flight, she began feeling very lightheaded and tried to shake that feeling off by requesting a glass of water from the hostess. While having her drink, she observed Che' and Link as they played a video game together. Father and son had developed a wonderful relationship that was filled with love, pride, and admiration for each other. Now she was fully convinced that moving back to England was the right thing to do for her family. Thinking about Mrs. Athien and Michelle always made her a little tense and angry; they had taken so much away from her, and she knew that there was a big fight ahead, but she was determined to be victorious for her son's sake. *No one will ever hurt or make him sad,* she silently vowed.

"Mommy, I beat Daddy at the car racing game—twice!" Link said.

She did not respond as sickness took over her body.

Che' looked at Akeila when she did not answer and thought that it was unusual; disregarding her son was not something that she had done in the past. When he saw her flushed face, he knew that something was terribly wrong. She looked pale, her eyes were weak, and she was perspiring greatly like she was about to pass out at any minute. "Akeila, baby, are you okay?" he asked, rushing to her side. When she did not respond but just stared at him with lifeless eyes, he quickly paged the airhostess and then gently wiped her face.

"Che', I do not feel good . . ." she whispered softly, and then she lost consciousness.

"Akeila, wake up!" Che' said frightfully, though he tried not to upset Link who was staring at his mom with concern and was about to cry. "Honey, wake up!"

"Mommy, Mommy!" Link cried, undoing the seat belt and then running quickly to his mother's side to hold her lifeless hand.

"Mommy will be okay," Che' said, reassuring his son. He wanted to take his small body in his arms and comfort him, but right now Akeila needed him more. Quickly he took the first aid kit from the air hostess and then applied some smelling salts to his wife's nose as they tried to revive her.

Akeila woke up to the soft whisper of her husband's voice, and she slowly opened her eyes. He regarded her with worry and concern while sitting next to her, with Link in his lap. He had carried her to the bottom deck and placed her in the bed.

"How do you feel?" he asked, taking her small hand.

"What happened?" she asked. She had no idea what had just happened and why they looked so troubled.

"You fainted for a few minutes," Che' replied, examining her face to make sure that she was all right.

"Are you better now, Mommy?" Link said softly.

"Yes, honey, Mommy is better now." She smiled to soothe him, and then she reached out and slowly ruffled his hair. "Just a little tired."

"I am tired too," Link whispered, yawning and then lying in the bed next to her. Akeila wrapped her arms around him, and within minutes they both fell fast asleep.

Che' stared at his wife and son sleeping peacefully in the bed, and he was very happy that he had the resources to make sure that they were comfortable. They were his family, and he loved them more than life itself. When Akeila passed out, he was very scared of losing her, and thoughts of her being sick and helpless petrified him. *Why did she faint?* he wondered. Was the thought of going back to England with him too overwhelming? Knowing that she had bad memories there only made him blame himself for not protecting her. He had failed her miserably in the past, but he certainly would not allow it to happen again. He yawned and then slowly reached out and tucked the blanket around them. A nap was what he needed, but he couldn't take it because his wife may need him if she woke up.

"Che'," Akeila whispered, softly rubbing her eyes.

"Hi, honey, how you feel?" he asked taking her hands as she focused her attention on him. He looked tired, and his eyes were red. They had been traveling for several hours and still had a few more to go.

"You should take a nap," she said, looking at him with concern.

"I can't. What if you get sick again?" he countered. "Who is going to take care of you?"

"There is no need to worry, honey. I am okay," Akeila insisted, trying to put his mind to rest.

"How can you say that? You just fainted," he responded, surprised by how calm she was. "We do not know the reason why."

"I understand what you are saying, honey, but—"

"Akeila, do you have any regrets about coming back to Woodstock with me?" he asked, interrupting her. "Is the prospect of going there too overwhelming for you? Is that the reason why you lost consciousness?"

"Honey," Akeila whispered. She reached out and touched his face. "You are my husband and the father of my son, and I love you. Where you are, that is where I want to be. Home is where you are."

Che' smiled as he saw their future in her eyes, and he believed every word as he kissed her fingers. "Why did you faint? Are you in pain?"

"I was thinking about England. It holds a lot of bad memories for me, but I know that things are going to be different this time around."

"I promise you that it will be," he said, nibbling on her finger.

"I have an idea as to the reason why I fainted."

"Why?" he asked, reaching out and caressing her face, eagerly anticipating the answer.

"I may be pregnant," she whispered softly while watching for his reaction.

"Pregnant?" he repeated, and his fingers abruptly paused on her face. He could not believe what he had just heard. He was going to be a father for the second time, and the prospect thrilled him.

"I have not had a period in three months," she said, never taking her eyes of him. "During my entire pregnancy with Link, I was very sick. I assumed that any other pregnancy that followed would be similar, but when it did not happen, I put my suspicions out of my mind."

"Three months, honey?" Che' inquired, deep in thought but never taking his hand away from her face. "That means that you got pregnant on your graduation night?"

"Yes, I believe that's when it happened. We made love more than once that night, and I do not recall using any protection," she added.

"I am sorry about that, because I wanted you so bad—and I still do," he whispered. Then he kissed her lightly on her lips. When the kiss deepened and he began nibbling on her tongue, she pulled away slowly.

"Baby," she purred, smiling seductive at him. "Please do not start something that you cannot finish."

"This is my private jet, and I can do whatever I desire," he said, smiling mischievously.

"Oh, really?" Akeila whispered, smiling playfully at him as she let her fingers travel slowly from his eyes to his lips, then down his chest and to his groin. "Go to sleep, husband," she said, laughing at his expression, which had changed from desire to surprise.

"Baby, look what you have done!" Che' groaned in frustration. His erection was quite visible.

"You are tired, honey, and we still have over two hours of flying left," she said with concern. "Come and lay down."

Che' looked at his wife, and as much as he desired her, he knew that she was right. They got very little sleep last night and rose before the sun, making the necessary preparations to leave. They were going to have another child, and he was ecstatic. "You are right my darling wife," he replied, getting in the bed and gently taking her in his arms as she snuggled close. "We will definitely finish that later."

Father, mother, and son slept until they landed and were awakened by the hostess. The early September weather in Woodstock England was comfortable, but there was a cool breeze blowing that made it seem much colder than it actually was. The weather was very unpredictable because of the climate change; winter was cold and wet and the summer was not as hot as New York. Akeila remembered when she arrived in the country for the first time and had experienced winter, which was horrible and bitterly cold. Her body was trembling and her teeth were chattering. Even though she was wearing a jacket, she felt naked. The tea did not calm her, and tears fell from her eyes. She recalled Che' wrapping her in his jacket and then taking her in his arms and carrying her to the car. She glanced at her husband and smiled when she comprehended that he had remembered the incident too.

Che' looked at his family, who was sitting next to him in the limousine. Link was very happy and excited as he looked through the car window. The changes were very fascinating to him, especially the security guard and the limousine driver. He asked was his dad was addressed as "sir." Che' laughed, explaining that he was a very important man. This was his family, and he silently vow to protect them from anyone or anything that had the potential to hurt or cause harm—even his own mother.

The Woodstock countryside was beautiful. Trees swayed in the wind, and the grass was lusciously green. There were fields with crops that were mostly harvested as farmers prepared for the upcoming winter. Farm animals like horses, cows, and sheep grazed on large pastures. Butterflies, black birds, and wild rabbits were present all around. As they drove deeper into the area where the wealthy resided, there was a drastic change in the scenery and atmosphere. The huge houses were exceptionally designed, and the landscapes and gardens were flawless. Most of the properties were gated and secured. Akeila always enjoyed driving through the area on days when she was overwhelmed with the pressures of life; viewing the scenery would always calm her. There was large acreage for horse riding and golfing on the estate. As they got closer, she became tenser.

"Akeila," Che' said, breaking her concentration as they pulled into the road leading to the entrance of the house. "Cover your eyes, please."

"Why, should I do that?" she asked with curiosity and concern in her eyes.

"I have a surprise for you."

"Do you have a surprise for me too, Daddy?" Link asked.

"Your surprise will come later, son," Che' replied. "Right now I need you to help me put this blindfold on your mommy."

"Okay, Daddy!" Link said excitedly. He was almost four and sometimes Che' is amaze by how intelligent he was. He spoke quite fluently and expresses himself very clearly in a way that kids much older than him does.

Minutes later Akeila followed her family, who led her into the unknown. After walking for a short time, Che' asked her to stand still.

"Open your eyes, Mommy," Link shouted happily as his father removed the blindfold.

"Oh my God, where am I?" she screamed when beholding the elegance that surrounded her. This house was exactly how she dreamed her perfect home could be. It was modern and sophisticated. Everything was detailed and harmonized perfectly, from the colors and themes to the furniture and decorations. "Where are we?"

"This is our home, Akeila," Che' replied, looking around the room with satisfaction. He gave the architect the ideas that he wanted the house to entail, but he never believed that it would have been built so perfectly detailed. The house was surrounding with luxury and that was what he wanted for his family.

"Che', we are on the estate; I know the route quite well," she answered with a puzzled look on her face. "How could this be our home?"

"It is the estate, but I had our own wing built," he said. "We will be able to live our life without interference from anyone."

"Oh my God, Che', it's beautiful. Thank you, honey!" she screamed, jumping into his arms and hugging him tightly. "Link, baby, this is our new home."

"Now it's time for *your* surprise, young man," Che' said, grabbing his son playfully and covering his eyes with his hands as he carried him. Akeila followed close behind, eagerly anticipating the surprise at hand.

They entered a lovely kid's room where the wall was stained with white and there was a blue curtain hanging in the window. The wooden floors were partly carpeted in sky blue, and there was a large plane crafted on the walls with Link's name written on it. There was a wooden, full-size white bed that was shaped in the form of a plane, and the bedding coordinated perfectly with the sky theme. The only furniture present was a desk, chair, computer, and a tall shelf filled with many books. Adjourning the bedroom was a huge playroom filled with toys that the average preschooler would enjoy, as well as educational materials posted on the walls.

"Thank you, Daddy," Link said, quickly hugging his father and then rushing toward the chest full of toys.

Che' and Akeila walked quietly arm in arm, observing and admiring the various rooms. The wing had six luxurious bedroom, three bathrooms rooms, a playroom, and a study. There was a huge living room, a kitchen, and a dining area.

"Thank you," Akeila whispered softly as they sat on a big, comfortable couch in the living room. She slowly reached out and hugged her husband, and then she lay in his arms.

"You and my son's happiness mean everything to me," he replied, hugging her tightly. When he saw how enthusiastic and joyful his family was when they saw their new home, it made him proud and elated to be the one who made it to happen.

"Words cannot express how happy I am."

"Honey, I can see it in your eyes and in your actions."

"When did you accomplish all of this?" she asked, letting her eyes travel all over the room.

"After we made love for the first time in New York, I realized that we belonged together. I called my contractor and

instructed him of the work that I wanted to have done," Che'
answered, very pleased with himself.

"Why didn't you say something?" she asked, smiling and
then kissing him quickly. "I love this house very much."

"I did not want to ruin the surprise, and you are welcome,"
he answered, looking at her intensely. He loved the way that
her brown eyes lit up when she smiled.

She asked, "Why are you looking at me like this?"

"Like what?"

"I can see desire in your eyes," Akeila said, blushing.

"Aren't you going to thank me properly?" Che' asked,
smiling roguishly as his hands began slowly massaging her
nipples, which rose from his touch.

"Later tonight," she said, jumping from his arms. "Right
this moment, I am absorbed with this house. I am going
exploring."

"Go ahead, honey, I have some work that I have to catch
up with," he said, gently tapping her on her butt. "I will be in
my study."

After feeding Link, Akeila gave him a bath, and soon after
he fell asleep while listening to the beginning of the story *The
Lion King*. She then entered the master bedroom, the last place
to explore, and her expectation was greatly met because it was
everything that she had visualized. There were walk-in closets,
a luxurious and modern bathroom, a king-size bed covered in
silk sheets, and a mounted TV on the white walls. The most
distinctive part of the area to her was the balcony. There was
an amazing view of the estate's topography and a man-made
pond that was surrounded with flowers and shrubs. The sky
was covered with stars, and there was a full moon that kissed
the trees as it shined. She thought about her husband and how
he'd made all this happened. He had used his resources to give
her a dream house that was so much more than she had ever
imagined. Finding out that he was a billionaire did not matter
much to her because she was in love with him, and that was

of utmost importance. His mom, however, alleged differently, believing that she was after his money. Akeila remembered Mrs. Athien's hurtful words the day that she paid off: "Stay away from my son! He is a very wealthy man, and I will not allow a gold-digging tramp like you to take advantage of him. You are not worthy enough to be the future of the Athien family. Take this money and disappear. Remember that if you ever come back, I will have you arrested for stealing." Those words still upset Akeila whenever she thought about it. However, presently she would not let that woman steal her joy. She would deal with her and any other problems tomorrow. All the excitement that followed when she saw their new home made her feel so vibrant and alive, even though they had traveled for hours. Saying a thank-you to Che' was not good enough for all that he had done for their family. It took a lot of planning, work, and money to have made their new home a reality, and she was going to find a way to express her gratitude. Suddenly an idea dawn on her, and she smiled triumphantly.

After reviewing some of the cases that were solved in his absence and formulating a few strategies on the new ones, Che' knew that it was time for him to go to bed. His mom had called a few times, but he did not answer the phone. He knew that it was only a matter of time before she came knocking, but he was too angry with her to have any kind of confrontation. He knew that she was curious in seeing the huge extension that was added to the main house. Men had been working twenty-four hours for the past three months to ensure that they got the job done to perfection. He still could not understand how cruel and abusive she had been toward his wife. He never thought that she was capable of hurting anybody to that extend, especially him. They had always had a great relationship and he loved her dearly, but that was why this whole situation was so painful.

His wife had served him a quick dinner in his office and left, not wanting to disturb him. His wife . . . The thought of Akeila waiting for him in his bed brought a smile to his face. He wondered if she was asleep, because someone in her condition who had just traveled from another continent would definitely be tired. He was going to be a father for the second time and was definitely going to share every moment this time around. He walked into his son's room, gently kissed him, and then gazed at his sleeping image with love and admiration. He slightly closed the door and walked over to the master bedroom, which was nearby.

When Che' got to his room, he was pleasantly surprised to see Akeila's silhouette by candlelight across the huge bed. She was scantily clothed in two pieces of black lingerie.

"Baby, why don't you go and take a shower?" she whispered, smiling seductively at him. "I would like to demonstration how happy you make me." She slowly bit on her fingertips while slightly opening her legs so that he could see a little of her half-clad, toned buttocks.

With his wife gazing at him with desire and hunger in her eyes, Che' quickly stripped, his erection visible as his need for her increased. "Your wish is my command," he whispered, and he rushed into the bathroom. Minutes later, he emerged naked and crawled into the bed, reaching for her.

"Easy, baby," Akeila purred, kissing him deeply and then slowly pushing him unto the pillow. Then she left the bed. "I will be right back."

Che's gaze followed Akeila as she walked across the room. The see-through lingerie clung tightly to her skin, and the matching high heel boots made her legs look longer. She put the stereo on, which he had built especially for her because of her love for music. The sweet music of Usher Raymond's "Making Love" filling the room, and he was really surprised when she began slowly dancing to the rhythm, her small waist gyrating slowly to the beat of the music. His desire ripened dramatically when she began stripping slowly, and her top fell to the ground. He watched as her nipples stood rigid and she stuck out her butt. He wanted to reach out and take them in his mouth. God, he wanted her so bad. His groin was so hard, and he was ready to take her. He felt like he was in a daze as his eyes feasted on her. He was overwhelmed with passion when she stood before him naked. She looked like a Greek goddess who had hypnotized him with her love. When he looked closer, he realized that her waist was a few inches thicker, and he was even more convinced that she was with child. His pregnant wife was strip dancing for him, and he wanted her right now. He could not bear it anymore, so he quickly got up, scooped her into his arms, and kissed her hungrily as he carried her to the bed.

"I am so sorry, baby," Che' said hoarsely, positioning himself above her. "I cannot wait any longer." She was wet as he drove into her. Akeila moaned and moved her waist to match his movements while they pleasured each other. They both climaxed, screaming each other's names. Soon after, they fell asleep peacefully in each other's arms.

CHAPTER 7

Akeila sat in her husband's study while reading up on posttraumatic stress. It was an illness that was common in solders who survived wars, violent crimes, and torture. They experienced these events that were catastrophic and, they were most likely to suffer from nightmares, detachment, disturbance of sleep, and memory loss. She had an interview for a job counseling veterans. Che' had made it possible, stating that because of her love for mankind, she would do a remarkable service that was greatly needed. She was very happy, and everything seemed to be perfect with their lives. The past two weeks had been amazing. Link had been enrolled in a very prestigious school, and even though he was almost four, he skipped prekindergarten after doing a placement test. They were so proud of him because the transformation was very easy. Che' had been working very hard on a terrorist case but always came home to have dinner with his family, although sometimes he had to go back to the job afterward. The doctors confirmed that Akeila was sixteen weeks pregnant, and she was starting to show a little but only when naked. Her husband was very attentive and caring, always calling to check up on her, and she did not complain. They had hired a maid and a chef to assist them with the maintenance of the house. At first she was reluctant, but he assured her that they needed extra help with a baby on the way, Link, and her new job.

She believed that it was only a matter of time before someone came around to dispute things and cause problems. She was knowledgeable of the fact that her mother-in-law had been calling Che' constantly, but she never inquired about their conversations. She did not want to bring up the topic of Mrs. Athien or Michelle even though they often crossed her mind. These two women had caused her so much pain and almost destroyed her marriage. She was still convinced deep in her heart that they still had the power to affect her happiness indirectly.

"Akeila? Oh, there you are!" Che' said, walking up to his wife and kissing her on the cheek.

"How was your day, honey?" she asked. "Did you catch the bad guys?"

"Almost. We have made a lot of progress in the case, and I believe that we will make an arrest soon," he said while sitting on the recliner next to her.

"I am so proud of you. I am a lucky woman. I have two intelligent men in my life."

"Thank you," Che' responded. He took the book from her hands and browsed through it with a sad expression on his face. "Posttraumatic stress is such a serious problem, and I am so happy that there are people who can help my fellow comrades."

"Yes, it is, but I am a little worried about the interview," she said. "This will be my first official job as a therapist."

"Don't worry, you will get the job. This country needs caring people like you to help, and besides, your husband is the chief of Homeland Security."

She looked at the clock on the desk. "Why are you home so early?"

"We are having guests over for dinner tonight," he said with a lack of enthusiasm in his voice, and then he looked away.

"Who is it?"

"My mother."

When Akeila remained silent, Che' regarded her and realized that she was worried. "You do not have to worry," he whispered softly. "You and I are a team, and from now on, we are going to handle our problems together."

"Okay, we will," Akeila said, smiling as she got up from the chair and began walking toward the kitchen.

"I have been trying to avoid my mother for the past three weeks. When she calls, I usually keep the conversation very short," he explained while following her to the kitchen. "I think it's time for her to know that you and Link are here."

"Are you telling me that you have not seen your mother yet?" she asked in disbelief.

"I have passed by the main house twice since we came back, but I only stayed a few minutes," he replied.

"How was it?"

"I did not say much, because I am still very upset with the way that she treated you," Che' replied as he sat at the kitchen table.

Akeila walk to the refrigerator, poured herself a glass of orange juice, and handed a beer to her husband before sitting next to him. She knew that this whole situation was not easy for him because of the love and respect that he had for his mother. *Did he see Michelle?* she wondered. She then looked at him with her eyes filled with many questions that she was afraid to ask.

"What's wrong, honey?" Che' asked when he saw that worried look on her face. He knew that his mom was not the only person that was on her mind. "I am going to see Michelle in an hour and have invited her to my office, where she will be informed that you and I are back together."

Akeila took a drink from her glass, not uttering a word while she listened. She knew that Che' loved her, but he had been engaged to Michelle twice now. If Akeila was not around, they would probably be together right now.

"I know that Michelle will be surprised when she learns that we are back together. With all her plotting and trickery, upon coming to the awareness that she has lost, there will be a big problem," he admitted.

"Do you think that she is going to accept the fact that we are back together?" Akeila asked, knowing that Michelle would not take defeat so easily.

"Honestly, I do not think that she will." He finished his beer. "It doesn't really matter if she does. The fact is that we are a family, and neither she nor my mother will ever come between us again.

"You promise, honey?" Akeila whispered softly, wanting so much for him to reassure her about their future.

"Akeila, look at me darling," Che' whispered, "You, Link, and this baby mean everything to me." When she looked into his eyes and saw the love that he had for his family she trusted him wholeheartedly; his eyes could never lied to her. Her family would definitely have to stand together as a unit if they wanted to be triumphant. Michelle and his mother were a very strong team.

"What's on the menu?" Akeila inquired with a smile.

"My mother loves Italian, but let's order in," Che' said, laughing as he walked over to her and began massaging her shoulders. "Baby, you are so tense."

"After informing me that your mom will be over for dinner and you are meeting Michelle, what do you expect?" she answered.

"Don't worry," Che' said, replacing his fingers with his lips as she giggled. "I will continue this later. Now, I have to go and help our son with his homework before leaving for the office."

"Link is home? Why didn't he come and say good afternoon to me?"

"I bought him a remote control plane to play with, so that I could have some private time to tell you about my mother coming over."

"Sneaky! Let me start making the necessary preparations for dinner," Akeila said, laughing as she walked toward the telephone.

Michelle hummed as she applied the last bit of makeup to her face. Everything looked perfect: she was dressed in a flowered sun dress, a yellow Juicy Couture blazer, and matching sandals. She headed to Che's office filled with confidence. When she had received the call from Che' a few hours ago, asking her to come over, she was thrilled at the prospect of being with him. She assumed that he was not angry with her anymore and had finally decided to set a day for their nuptials. The last time that they were together, there was a big fight that led her to believe that she may have lost him. Akeila, his ex-wife whom she hated with a passion, was the cause of that disagreement. In her mind she knew that there was no reason for her to be jealous of that simple woman, but her heart was telling her differently. The way that Che' looked at Akeila and catered to her needs had convinced her over the years that he loved her dearly, and that was where Michelle's jealousy and resentment stemmed from. She always believed that Che' would be there waiting to love her, but when Akeila came into his life, the reality was that she was greatly mistaken. All the effort that was place in seducing him and getting his attention was unsuccessful, and that was when it dawned on her that she had lost him forever. This was a reality that she was never going to accept. She needed to get rid of her competition and had eventually been effective in doing so. With her lavish lifestyle, she was living beyond her means, so when the bank had informed her that she was broke, it did not come as a surprise. They wanted her to file for bankruptcy, which was not an option. She did not want to draw such negative publicity to herself because her reputation meant everything to her. She was considered one of the most beautiful models in England, and she wanted her status to remain unblemished. As a model, the jobs had gotten fewer over the years, and her agent have not called in months; no one wanted a model who was forty-three, he'd pointed out. She wanted Che' Athien to marry her desperately, but she needed his money even more.

When she entered his office, he was sitting at his desk with a vague expression on his face. The scene was not at all what she had expected.

"Have a seat," Che' said formally, not making any effort to greet her personally.

"Well, hello to you too, darling," she said sarcastically, realizing that something was wrong. She moved close to him with a smile on her face and then reached out to kiss him, but he quickly got out the way and walked toward the door, opening it slightly. "What's wrong, darling? Are you still mad at me?"

"I am not mad at you, Michelle. That's why I wanted to talk to you," Che' said as he walked back to his chair.

"Does this means that things are back to normal?" Michelle asked as happiness beamed in her blue eyes. "Darling—"

"Michelle, it is over," Che' blurted out when he realized that she misunderstood the whole situation. The only reason why he wanted to meet with her was because he believed that he owed her an explanation. He wanted nothing further to do with her afterward because of the unscrupulous way that she had treated his wife. He simply wanted closure.

"What did you say?" she asked with surprise in her voice. "We can't be over."

"This relationship has been over for quite some time now," he said unemotionally.

"How can you say that it's over, Che'? Why?" She walked toward him. "Darling, we are good for each other. We are from the same social class, and can you imagine all the things that we can do together?"

Che' looked at Michelle with contempt in his eyes. He hated the pathetic woman and wondered what he had ever seen in her. She tried so hard to look younger than her forty-three years by wearing makeup and clothes that were not age appropriate. The full-coverage makeup that she had on her face made her look unreal.

"Find someone who can make you happy, because we have no future together," Che' said softly while looking at his watch.

"I want no one else, Che," she pleaded as tears fell from her eyes. "Darling, we can start over."

"No, we can't," he replied as his anger began to surface. This conversation was so much longer than he had anticipated. All that he wanted to do right now was to get home to his family.

"Why not? We did it before, and it was good."

"Michelle it's over. I do not love you."

"No, it is not! I know that I can make you love me again," Michelle stuttered as she walked toward him and fell at his feet, sobbing.

"Michelle, stop this nonsense and have some pride," he shouted angrily, immune to her tears. At first they made him feel sorry for her, but over the years he realized that she would use them as a tool to get whatever she wanted. He had to strongly convince her that they did not have a future together. "My wife is back."

"What did you just say?" Michelle asked, jumping quickly to her feet with all of her tears magically disappearing.

"Akeila and I are back together," Che' answered, observing her closely.

Hearing the name Akeila made Michelle overwhelmed with anger. "You took that bitch back after all that she has done to you!" she yelled.

"Please do not call my wife names in my presence," he warned her with anger in his eyes. "I am quite aware of the role that you played in making her unhappy and destroying my marriage."

Michelle knew that he was furious, but she did not care. The realization that he knew about her deceitfulness did not prevent her from pleading her case. She was not going to lose him to Akeila again. "Don't you see? She does not fit into our world—she is a nobody!" Then she saw a picture of Akeila and a little boy that looked like Che' on his desk. Consumed with envy and rage, she grabbed the picture and held it out to him. "You took that tramp and her bastard son back!"

"Get out of my office, or I will have you thrown out!" Che' ordered, firmly grabbing the picture out of her hands. "If you ever call my son a bastard again, or if you even come close to my family, you will have to answer to me."

Michelle looked at Che' and realized that this was not a useless threat. He had a deadly look on his face, like a solder in battle fighting for his honor. He frightened her, and she knew that being around him was not in her best interests. "I hate you, Che' Athien!" she screamed, rushing to the door. "You will regret treating me in this manner!" Then she walked away. With rage and jealousy in her heart, she dialed his mother, who was always there for her. She did not believe that the old lady was aware Akeila was back, because Mrs. Athien would have informed her as soon as she became knowledgeable of the fact. After receiving no answer, she quickly got in her car and drove to the only place where she was free to be herself.

"How could he do this to me?" she screamed, punching the couch that was close by. She then threw the pillows and anything that was within range across the room as pain and disappointment overwhelmed her.

"Did what?"

Michelle turned around slowly, recognizing Franko's voice as he stood in front of the open door, observing the messy room. She had used his spare keys to enter his home and was very happy to see him. He never judged her and always had the power to make her feel hopeful when she seemed lost. It did not matter what her problems may be; he was always there, offering resolutions. While she had been drowned in her sorrow, she did not notice him opening the door. She ran quickly into his arms and started sobbing.

"Don't cry, darling. Why don't you sit down and tell me what's wrong?" He led her to a chair. He hated seeing crying, vulnerable women because it reminded him of his mother, who had been abused by men all her life.

"He took her back!"

"Who are you talking about?" Franko asked, trying to understand why she was so upset. Over the past few months he had develop strong feelings for her. She seemed to connect to his dark side, was never judgmental, and always understood his devious intentions. He loves that about her.

"Che'! He took that bitch back!" she shouted in anger.

When Franko heard Che's name, his curiosity increased even more. This may be the ammunition that he had been waiting for all these years. He had to approach this conversation with caution in order to get the information that he desired. "Who did he take back?" he probed.

"Akeila, his wife," she spat.

"I did not know that he had a wife. I thought that he was divorced."

"Well, it seems that he never divorced her. I do not understand what he sees in her. They have nothing in common; they are from different cultures, social classes, and families. He left all those sophisticated, cultured women in England and went to a third-world country to find a bride."

"Why did he take her back?" he asked.

"He claims that he loves her. Loves her! After all the work that his mom and I put in to making her disappear—it was all in vain," she added.

"What do you mean?"

"His mother never approved of the marriage. She made Akeila's miserable when she was living on the estate. We led Che' to believe that his wife ran off with a secret lover, stealing a large sum of his money in the process. Then we made her think that *he* was unfaithful," Michelle replied, not in the least bit regretful of what she did.

"Clever plot, darling. I am very impressed," Franko replied, smiling approvingly. He could not have concocted a better plan for that kind of situation.

"Not so clever after all. He never stopped loving her, and now they are back together," she replied indignantly. "Do you know that they have been together for the past few months?"

"Is that where he was when you were trying to get in contact with him?" Franko asked as he tried putting together the pieces of his enemy's life.

"Yes, that's where he was," Michelle said crossly, "With that bitch and her son!" Finding out that Akeila was pregnant was by accident. Michelle had gone to the doctor on that day for her yearly checkup and was surprised when she saw Akeila there talking to the doctor. As she eased herself closer to listen to their conversation, she heard the doctor congratulating Akeila on the pregnancy. She knew that a baby would make it impossible for Che' to leave his wife, knowing how much he wanted to have children. There had to be a way to prevent Akeila from telling Che' about his baby, and she cleverly found it. She called his mother, who was very happy to assist her. Seducing him was not as easy, but her task was complete when she made sure that Akeila saw her kissing her husband even though he quickly pushed her away. After all this work in conspiring and scamming, she would not lose what rightfully belonged to her: Che' Athien and all his millions. She would have to find a way to get rid of Akeila permanently.

Franko felt as though he had won the lottery. He had finally found Che' Athien's weak point, his family. From the anger and resentment that he saw blazing in Michelle's eyes anytime she mentioned the wife's name, he concluded that his nemesis loved her dearly. Che' had taken a chance in marrying an outsider, making her a part of his empire, and having an heir. That was the type of love that people read about in story books. Even though Franko had never experienced that type of love, it did not matter to him. The only love he had in his heart was for his family, and he could finally avenge their deaths. He loved being in the company of different women, but for now Michelle seemed to satisfy him greatly. He observed her as she stared at the walls, and he concluded that she was formulating some Machiavellian plan in her mind. His plot was even more Machiavellian—and deadly. He admired the fact that she did whatever it took to get what her heart desired, and it turned him on. He gently scooped her up and carried her to the bed, where their lovemaking was fueled by hatred and vengeance.

CHAPTER 8

"Mommy, why are we dressing up to have dinner at home?" Link asked while buttoning his white long-sleeve shirt, which matched perfectly with his black skinny jeans and black shoes. Akeila regarded her son with love and pride in her heart. Sometimes she would forget how old he was because of his maturity and the questions that he asked. Every day he seemed to resemble his dad more and more. He had adjusted perfectly into his new environment and was a very happy little boy.

"We are going to have a very special guest over for dinner tonight," Akeila replied as she brushed his hair.

"Who is coming to dinner, Mommy?"

"It's your grandmother, sweetheart," she answered softly, observing her son closely. After all the verbal abuse and humiliation that she had suffered at the hands of this woman, she would make sure that her son would not go through the same thing. She would do whatever it took to protect him.

"Wow, Mommy! Grandma and Grandpa are coming to see our new home?" Link added excitedly. "Are Aunty Pam and Aunty Tasha coming too?"

She placed her son on her lap as she explained. "Baby, it's Daddy's mother, your other grandmother."

"Okay, I am going to have two grandmothers," he said, smiling. "That's awesome, Mommy."

Che' walked into his son's room and saw his wife ruffling his hair as he giggled. His heart was overflowing with love for them. They were his family, the most important thing in his life. His mom was a part of his family too. Even though she was a complicated woman, he loved her very much, and that was the reason why, when he found out about her role in Akeila's disappearance, he was greatly disappointed. When his dad died, he was a teenager, and she adjusted to the role of both parents quite perfectly. Although there was help, she had always put him first, and he always felt her love. The only problem that he knew that she had was handling money; she was a shopaholic and gambled. His dad and grandmother wanted to secure the family finances, so they left 90 percent of the estate to him after they'd died. His mother had no problem with the will; in fact, she had access to everything. Giving her another chance was something that he knew he had to do, despite everything that she had done. He looked at Akeila and smiled. *Who could hate her?* he wondered. She was beautifully clad in a long, flowing, strapless black dress that hugged her body and showed of her slightly visible belly. She also wore black high-heel shoes, her makeup was naturally done, and her long hair fell over her shoulders. He walked over to them, scooped his son into his arms, and playfully kissed his cheeks as he giggled.

"Baby, you look gorgeous," he said to Akeila, and she blushed. He loved it when she did that because it reminded him of when they fell in love.

Moments later the doorbell rang. Che' had given the staff the evening off, and so he quickly went to answer it. He did not know what would happen over dinner, but he wanted it to remain in the family. His mom had no idea that Akeila was back; he'd arranged it in such a way that Michelle would not be able to inform his mother after he officially broke it off with her. Mrs. Athien usually played bridge with her friends around that time and never picked up the phone. The new wing also had its own entrance, and the family limousine was dark and private, so it was impossible for her to see anyone when they left the house. He stood in front of the door and then turned and looked at his wife while Link left the room, playing with his remote control plane.

"Are you ready, Akeila?" he asked softly as he examined her face.

"As ready as I can be," she replied. Then she walked toward the dining room as Che' opened the door and let his mother in.

"Good afternoon, Mother," he said, greeting her with a kiss on her cheek. "Let me take your jacket."

"Good evening, son," she replied, hugging him as she entered inside the house.

The cold fall breeze blew through the open door, giving the room a cool, refreshing feeling. Most of the trees had already lost their leaves, and it was shaping up to be a very cold winter. "You have a very beautiful home, son," Mrs. Athien added as she curiously gazed at her surroundings. "The design is immaculate, and the interior decorating is exceptional and contemporary."

"Shall I take you for a tour, Mother?" he asked, smiling as he led her toward the other rooms.

Akeila stood in the dining room and then slowly began pacing the floor. *What is taking them so long?* she said to herself. Then she nervously started to arrange the already perfect china. The maid and chef had done a remarkable job of preparing the food and decorating the table. The crystal was a floral design and matched perfectly with the white cloth napkins. The huge gemstone chandelier, which was the main attraction in the area, made the china shine even more. "Where is every one?" she whispered in aggravation. Even Link was nowhere to be found.

Mrs. Athien said, "Son, you have done a wonderful job. This house is amazing. Even though your contractor was rude and impolite, he is excellent at what he does."

Akeila heard the voice and knew to whom it belonged. She remembered vividly that voice provoking her, cursing her, and laughing at her. She waited nervously for them to enter the room, and when they did she stood there motionless, staring at her mother-in-law. The old lady had aged gracefully; her hair had turned grey and was stylishly pinned in a bun. She had gained a few pounds and was neatly clothed in a designer blue suite. She gazed at her son with love and admiration in her eyes while talking about the house.

"Thank you, Mother. I am happy that you approve," Che' replied as he gazed at Akeila across the room.

"As much as I love this house, the main house is not the same without you," Mrs. Athien said softly, looking at her son with loneliness in her eyes. "It was not necessary for you to get a new home; there is enough room for you, Michelle, and the grandchildren that I am longing for."

"Mother, there is something that I need to tell you," Che' said. "My—"

"Son, this dining room is beautiful. Where did you buy that chandelier?" she asked, walking over to inspect the china. "And those . . ." Then she paused with her mouth open in shock when she saw at Akeila standing there.

"Hello," Akeila greeted with a smile on her face, knowing that she had to get along with her mother-in-law for her husband's sake.

"What is *she* doing here?" Mrs. Athien yelled as she recovered from the shock.

"Mother, I think that you should have a seat," Che' said gently, taking her hand. He tried to lead her to a chair.

"I do not need to sit down, not until you explain what this girl is doing here!" she snapped, brushing away his hand.

"Mom, Akeila and I are back together. I love her and do not wish to live my life without her," he said softly, watching his wife.

"Garbage, son!" she replied, sitting down in the chair and continuing to glare at Akeila.

"Mother, that's the truth, and there is nothing you can do about it. I know about all the horrible things that you did to my wife and the part you played in driving her away. However, I am willing to put this behind me," he said calmly. "I love you, but if I have to choose, my family will definitely come first."

"Son, you and Michelle belong together!" Mrs. Athien insisted.

"No, we do not. I have already talked to Michelle, so it is in your best interest to accept things for what they really are," Che' said.

Akeila observed her mother-in-law and was not surprised by the woman's behavior, but her heart reached out to her husband, who was caught between the women that he loved. She became very upset when she recognized that his mother was not trying to meet him halfway.

"I will never accept her!" Mrs. Athien shouted furiously, pointing at Akeila with resentment in her eyes.

"Whether or not you consent to my wife does not change the way that things are," Che' replied as he started to get upset. "I am only trying to include you in the part of my life that means everything to me, so it's up to you."

Mrs. Athien looked at her son and saw the seriousness in his eyes, and it scared her. She knew that he was very serious about everything that he said. Her love for him was great, and she could not imagine her life without him. Then her eyes shifted to Akeila, who was the only woman to succeed, for the second time, in being top priority in her son's life. *What is so special about Akeila?* she wondered.

"Is that my grandma?" Link asked excitedly, rushing into the room and into the old lady's arms. Akeila looked at Mrs. Athien, who turned many shades of red when he sat in her lap. She was shocked and speechless. "Grandma, my name is Link," he said, smiling at her.

Mrs. Athien gazed at the kid sitting on her lap. He was around four and was a perfect replica of her son at that age. She was not aware that Akeila had been pregnant when she'd left, and the thought saddened her. This little boy was her grandson. With trembling fingers she gently touched his face and hair in order to convince her that he was real. With tears rolling down her face, she tightly kissed and hugged him.

"Why are you crying, Grandma?" Link asked softly, wiping the tears from her eyes with his small hand.

"I am so happy to meet you, honey," she said, joining him as they dried her tears. "Tell me, Link, how old are you, and what is your favorite meal?"

"I am almost four years old, Grandma, and I love chicken nuggets," he replied, smiling excitedly.

While the two got acquainted, Che' and Akeila watched them in disbelief. Mrs. Athien held Link tightly in her arms as he answered her questions happily. They never imagined that kind of reaction from this situation. A few minutes ago, the room had been filled with a hateful battle of words, but now a child seemed to prove that victory was on the horizon.

"Grandma, do you want to see my room?" Link asked, pulling her to her feet.

"After dinner, son," Che' said softly, and he led everyone to the table. They ate their meal, Link and Mrs. Athien chatted. She wanted to find out everything about him, and when he informed her of his love for planes, she was happy to inform him that his grandfather was a collector of them. A wonderful bond connected the two. After dinner they went to his room while Che' and Akeila cleared the table.

The moon and stars shone brightly, which made the leafless trees look like creatures in a scary movie. There were a few fall flowers that the gardeners had planted to give the area a lovely sight. Everything seemed very peaceful and tranquil on the outside as Akeila stared through the window. She wanted to be alone with her thoughts but did not have that luxury, because her husband walked up behind her and gently wrapped his arms around her waist, drawing her closer. They remained in silence for a moment, deep in their own thoughts as they drew strength from each other.

"Baby, I am so sorry that my mom spoke to you in that manner," Che' said softly, breaking the silence as he nuzzled her hair, which smelled like raspberries from the shampoo that she had used.

"That's okay, honey. There was nothing that you could have done about it," Akeila said, smiling at him. "I am very impressed with the way that you handled this situation, especially the amount of patience that you have exercise."

"She is my mom, and I love her; that cannot change," he said, breathing deeply. "What I am greatly surprised by was the way that she embraced our son."

"I am still speechless about the way that she responded to him," Akeila admitted.

"Who could resist our little boy?" Che' added, smiling while turning her around so that he could look into her eyes. "I am so happy that she accepted him."

"Me too, honey, because if she did not, God knows that there was definitely going to be a big problem," Akeila said softly. She was going do whatever it took to protect her little boy. "Che', you would have been caught in the middle, and I do not want that for you."

"I do hope that one day my mother will see how wonderful and caring you are—and most important, how happy you have made me. I love you, Akeila. You are the best mother and wife, and you complement me perfectly."

"Honey, I know that this situation is not easy for you and my heart feels for you," Akeila said softly while gazing into his dark eyes. "You, Link, and this baby are my future, and I promise you that together we can survive everything. I love you."

"Say it again, Akeila."

"I love you."

"Oh, honey, I love you so much," Che' whispered, and their lips meet in a slow, gentle kiss. As the kiss grew deeper, Akeila wrapped her arms around his neck and molded her body into his.

"Excuse me, please."

Che' and Akeila drew apart when they realized that they were not alone. "Can I help you, Mother?" he asked.

"My grandson fell asleep after I read him a story—actually, he read it to me," she said, smiling. "I could not believe it when he did. He is an intelligent little lad."

"Yes, he is," Che' replied proudly. "Even though Link is only four, he is at a six-year-old level."

"Wonderful! He is my little genius. Well, I'd better be on my way now. Can I visit him tomorrow?"

"You can see him anytime, Mother," Che' answered, smiling as he walked toward her. "I will escort you home."

"Mrs. Athien, thank you for coming and for being so kind to my son," Akeila said confidently.

"He is a wonderful boy, and you two should be proud," Mrs. Athien said while looking at the two. "He told me that he has a sister on the way. Congratulations." When she walked away, there were tears falling from her eyes.

"Akeila, I will be back soon," Che' whispered, and then he quickly went to comfort his mother.

Akeila went to her son's room and kissed his cheeks while he lay peacefully sleeping. His presence had brought a silver lining behind that mountain of dark clouds, and she was thankful. Then the biblical scriptures that stated "a child shall lead the way" came to mind and brought a smile to her face. She slowly walked into her bedroom and dialed her family's telephone numbers. She informed them about everything that had occurred. Soon afterward she fell asleep with hope and faith in her heart.

After kissing her son goodnight, Mrs. Athien walked into her leaving room and ordered a nightcap. She then slowly retrieved a family album that was neatly arranged on her coffee table and sat down. She browsed through the pictures of her ancestors and then came across a picture of her husband and young son. Che' was sitting on his daddy's lap, looking at him with respect and admiration in his eyes. The picture was filled with love and pride from father to son. While looking at the pictures, tears fell from her eyes. Her family thrived on love, and somewhere along the way she had lost sight of that, and she believed that they would be greatly saddened by her behavior. When did she become so hateful and cruel? Her actions and deceit caused her pregnant daughter-in-law to leave with no plan. Now, her grandson was the future of the Athien family and the spitting image of her beloved Che'. The tears fell even harder when it dawned on her that she had almost missed the opportunity of having her only grandchild in her life, but faith had brought him back. She was not willing to make the same mistake again, and she wished for a second chance to make things right with her family.

The image of Che' and Akeila when she walked in on them after dinner came to mind. After taking the time to scrutinize them closely while they gazed into each other's eyes, she realized that they were madly in love. The love that they shared could be felt across the room. It reminded her of that time when her husband was alive, and they were madly in love. They were so happy, and she held those memories very dear to her heart. "Please forgive me, husband," she whispered softly while looking at his picture. She thought about her daughter-in-law and recognized that although she was unlike any of the women that her son had dated, she made him happy and would always be a part of his life. There was a baby on the way now, and Mrs. Athien had to do whatever it took to make it up to them.

Suddenly her cell phone rang, and she looked at the caller ID. It was Michelle, who had influenced her greatly in the vendetta against her son's wife. If she had given Akeila the opportunity to prove herself instead of letting her pettiness and other people's opinions crowd her judgment, things would have turned out differently. She did not want to be disturbed and refused to take the call. The only thing on her mind was trying to find a way to make it up to her family.

CHAPTER 9

The weather changed from a stiffening breeze to bone-chilling winds. Although December was one of the coldest months in Woodstock, there were still many people on the streets shopping and making the necessary preparations for the Christmas holidays. As the season changed, so did life for the Athien family in the months that followed. Che' sat in his office chair smiling to himself. Life was wonderful, and he was very happy with every aspect of it. He had done an excellent job as the chief of Homeland Security. He and his team caught the group of terrorists who wanted to bomb the English subway. His hard work earned him a medal from the Crown and praises from the prime minister and other high-ranking officials.

His duties as a father and husband were not neglected, either. On weekends he would take his son to little league hockey or any other extracurricular activities. He gave Link a glamorous four-year-old birthday party with a theme of his choice, and he was rewarded with his son's happiness. His mother's relationship with Akeila had improved greatly. She would come over to the house twice a week to play with Link, and they had dinner every Sunday with her. He was greatly impressed with his wife, who was doing an extraordinary job as a psychologist. She had a very caring heart for her patients that made her office a safe haven for the mentally distressed. The pregnancy was progressing wonderfully. She did not carry very big, and at seven months she was still very active. Che' smiled once more, thinking of the first time that he saw the sonogram of his baby daughter. Amazement and joy filled his heart when he heard her heartbeat and saw her move. The holidays were almost here, and he was eagerly anticipating it because it was the first one they were going to spend together as a family.

Thoughts of building a snowman with his son were interrupted by the buzzing of his intercom. When his secretary informed him that Michelle was here to see him, he hesitated but let her in. Since their agreement in his office month ago, he had not seen her or spoken to her. Even though she had called his cell phone several times, he had refused her calls.

"Good afternoon, Michelle. Please sit down," he greeted politely, wondering what her reason was for coming to see him. "How can I help you?"

"Why so formal, Che'? We shared so much, darling, and we have a history together," Michelle said, smiling as she flirted with him.

Che' remained quiet. Although Michelle was a gorgeous woman, her blue eyes looked lifeless and cold, like a statute. With her perfectly made up face and body clad with designer clothes, she looked beautiful; however, he pitied her. Although her life was filled with an abundance of material possessions, she seemed very empty and unhappy. "What can I do for you?" he repeated. He started to regret his decision in letting her in.

"I just wanted to say hello and see how you were doing," she said. "Darling, we have not seen or spoken to each other in a very long time."

"I am doing well."

"I can see that you are," she noted, observing his body with admiration. "I saw you on the television a few weeks ago, and commendations are in order for a job well done. Che', I am very proud of you."

"Thank you," he said softly, still trying to figure out the main reason for her visit.

"I would also like to apologize to you for my actions the last time that we saw each other. I am so embarrassed about the way that I have behaved," Michelle said, standing up and walking toward the door.

Che' got up and quickly opened the door to let her out. To his great surprise, Michelle threw her arms tightly around his neck, hugging him. He swiftly pulled away. "Good-bye, Michelle. Good luck with everything," he said.

"Thank you, and good-bye," she replied, smiling before walking away.

Che' closed the door and walked to the windows. He was on the fifth floor in a fifty-story building, and the view was very lovely. Cars and pedestrians were busy moving on the streets below, but the snow flurries were of more interest to him. They fell slightly but constantly against the office window. The virgin snow always made him think about purity and goodness. This was his favorite part of the winter season, and he couldn't wait to share it with his son.

However, his mind kept taking him back to Michelle's visit and he could not shake an uneasy feeling that something was definitely wrong. Knowing that she still did not accept his marriage to Akeila, he'd broken all dealings with her. She was always a vengeful person who did not take defeat easily. Today, however, she seemed very calm and confident, and she had a victorious gleam in her eyes that was definitely out of character. She probably had some hidden agenda, and he was now cognizant of it and would keep an eye on that woman, even considering her to be a threat.

Michelle drove her black Rolls Royce to the Athien estate. This lovely home was her dream house, and she had always considered it her home. While growing up she had been very privileged and had everything that an only child could have. She went to the best schools and socialized with the rich and famous. Although her parents were still alive, she had not seen them in years. She would call regularly but never seemed to have the time to visit them. They had no knowledge of her financial situation because she had received a trust fund years ago with millions of dollars. The knowledge that she was broke would definitely leave them speechless and very disappointed in her. She could not allow that to happen because they always considered her to be their princess who could do no wrong. If things went as planned, hopefully she would be able to visit soon—and in the process bring them something that they'd always wanted. If she had a wealthy husband, then her being broke would not be an issue.

The snow flurries started to stick on the ground, making the commute very messy and dangerous; however, she was in good spirits. Che' Athien was deeply on her mind and heart. She could still smell his cologne and feel his strong arms when she hugged him. He looked so handsome in his black designer suit, white shirt, and black tie. His black hair had grown a little since she'd last seen him, and his fathomless eyes made him look mysterious and dangerous. God, he was handsome, and she missed him terribly. She longed for his kisses and his touch. There had been many lovers in her life, but the only one that gave her sexual satisfaction and real love was Che'. He was the only man that she could not have wrapped around her fingers and who never fell for her trickery. His wealth and power made him even more irresistible, and she could not picture a life without him. She had tried to move on without him but couldn't. Franko was a very good diversion, but that's all he would ever be to her. He was not the type of guy that she could introduce to family and friends, or even be seen in public with. He did not fit into her social class, and neither did he possess any of the qualities that related to people of her caliber. The fact that he was a criminal did not frighten her. In fact, she loved the thrill of living on the edge, and he never judged her in spite of how evil her intentions were sometimes. The money and the sex were great, but all that he would ever be to her was a sweet secret. She pulled up to the house, quickly got out of her car, and buzzed the doorbell. She was greeted politely by the butler, who announced her arrival.

"Hello, Michelle," Mrs. Athien said, hugging and kissing her cheeks. "I did not expect to see you today."

"Hi, Mom," Michelle replied, kissing her wrinkled cheeks. "I wanted my visit to be a surprise. After all, you do not have time for me anymore."

"It's a pleasant surprise, and you will always be very dear to me," she replied, leading her into the sitting room. "How are you doing, honey?"

"I am doing great!" Michelle responded with fake enthusiasm. "I just came from Che's office, and we are getting back together."

Mrs. Athien looked at the lovely blonde woman sitting on the expensive couch, and her heart reached out to her. It suddenly hit her that Michelle was probably deluded or even crazy. During these past few months, Mrs. Athien had dealt with Michelle's mood swings, outbursts of tears, and accusations of betrayal, but she refused to be a tool in the vendetta against Akeila. She had offered monetary support and even the services of a therapist in order for Michelle to forget Che' and his family. She had believed that her friend was doing well, but now it seemed like that was not the case. All the proof was in her actions and the evil look that she had in her eyes.

"Michelle darling, my son is very happy with his family," she said gently. "He has a baby on the way now and will never leave them."

"Che' will never leave Akeila?" Michelle laughed. "Maybe she will be the one who leaves—permanently."

"What is that supposed to mean?" Mrs. Athien asked defensively. She thought of Akeila, who had become such a big part of her life. The time that they spent together was very important, and she'd learn to love and respect Akeila. She was starting to understand why her son loved his wife so dearly, and she did not want anything to happen to her. Her daughter-in-law was a wonderful mother and wife; she had heard that she was an excellent therapist too. "Darling, I think that you should really see a shrink."

"Don't patronize me, Mom!" Michelle screamed. "I am fine! Che' and I belong together. I love him, and he loves me too. Didn't you want us to be together? Well, now you are going to get what you have always wanted—me as your daughter-in-law!"

Mrs. Athien looked at the fury in Michelle's eyes, and it worried her. That woman was delusional and living in a fantasy world. Long ago, she wanted her to be Che's wife and the mother of his kids, truly believing that was the best choice for him. Now she realized the error of her thinking, and she was very grateful that he had disregarded her wishes. This woman was obsessed with her son, and that type of obsession was deadly and dangerous if it was not treated.

"I am very sorry, Mother," Michelle said cunningly when she realized that her former champion was looking at her with uncertainty in her frail eyes. She needed the old woman as her ally and had to find a way to remove any doubts that now existed in Mrs. Athien mind. "I love Che' so much," she sobbed, throwing herself on the couch as tears burst from her eyes.

"Michelle, you have to let him go," Mrs. Athien whispered, taking her friend's sobbing body in her arms while impiety filled her heart. "Why don't you get some professional counseling in order to move on?"

"I know that you are right. I really need help and support in getting over your son. Please help me, Mom," she whispered softly. "Why don't you call the shrink that you have recommended and make an appointment for me?"

"That's wonderful, darling, to make that first step," Mrs. Athien said, smiling with relief as she rushed to the phone. She had always cared about Michelle and wanted desperately for her to be happy. Most important, however, she wanted Michelle to leave her son's family alone and concentrate on making one for herself. "Dinner will be served in a few minutes, so why don't you join me?"

"Thank you, Mom, that's wonderful. I will be in the guest room freshening up. Please call me when dinner is ready," Michelle said as she climbed the staircase, smiling triumphantly. Now the old woman was exactly where she wanted her to be: clueless about her plans that were already in motion.

Akeila read the last page of the *Curious George* storybook and then kissed her sleeping son on his forehead. He'd had a long day and was very tired and fell asleep before the story ended. After picking him up from school, she took him to her job where he stayed for about three hours, and then they headed home. She pulled the blanket over his small body and walked slowly toward her bedroom. After dinner Che' had gone to have a nightcap with his mother, so Akeila took a long bath and started preparing for bed. She sat on the bed wrapped in her robe and started the difficult task of moisturizing her body. Her growing tummy made it difficult to lotion from her waist downward. The baby was resting very quiet, which was rare since she was usually very active, kicking and floating around. The only time when she was quiet was after her mom had eaten. Christmas was approaching, and she was greatly looking forward to it. She enjoyed shopping for presents, putting up the Christmas tree, and cooking lots of different foods. Her family in Grenada had welcomed a new addition. Pam had given birth to a healthy baby boy a few days ago, and everyone was celebrating this long-awaited birth. Thinking about them always puts a smile on her face, and the knowledge that they would be visiting her in the New Year was something to look forward to. She poured a little cream and slowly started to try getting to her feet. God it was so impossible, since she couldn't see her feet.

"Do you need some help?" Akeila looked up and saw Che' standing in front of the bedroom door with a big grin on his face.

"You know that I am in dying need for your assistance, honey," she replied smiling. "Are you enjoying the view?"

"Of my pregnant wife struggling to cream her feet? You bet I am," he laughed as he walked toward her.

"What is so funny?" she asked. "You should try carrying this baby, and then maybe you would understand what I have to go through." She then quickly threw the bottle playfully toward him. He caught it and then came over to assist by removing her robe.

"What are you doing?" Akeila asked. She did not protest when his fingers began caressing her nipples. He then carried his hand and rested it tenderly on her tummy.

"She is so quiet," Che' added with love and amazement on his face. There were times when the baby would kick so hard that he could feel it when laying close to his wife. He slowly let his fingers travel from her tummy to between her legs. "Che'," Akeila whispered breathlessly, leaning into him.

"Yes, honey," he replied huskily while caressing her inner thighs.

"You are not done moisturizing my body yet," Akeila purred as she kissed him.

"It can wait. Right now I want to pleasure my wife and then put her to bed," Che' replied with a roguish spark in his eyes. He quickly removed his clothes.

Che' laid Akeila gently unto the bed and then slowly kissed and caressed her body. He had to be very gently because of her advanced pregnancy. When they came together it was wonderful, and in the aftermath of their lovemaking they talked about the upcoming holidays.

"What would you like to have for Christmas?" Akeila asked while she played with the hair on his chest.

"I have everything that I want, here in this house," he whispered. "You, Link, and this baby are everything that I have ever dreamed of."

"We have so many differences, yet we are making it work," she replied softly.

"From the moment that I saw a young, lovely damsel tumbling down a few steps, I knew that she was the one for me," he said kissing her hair.

"Oh really, is that so?' Akeila said, tilting her head so that she could look into his eyes. "You knew from that moment that I was the one?"

"Yes my love, from that moment on, I saw you in my future. I did not see race, culture, or social class," Che' murmured folding his arms protectively around her shoulders. "I saw you, my princess, I saw you."

"I love you so much, honey, and we have wasted so much time," Akeila said softly. "These past four years . . ."

"Hush, we have both learned from that horrible experience. Now we know how very precious our love is, and we will do whatever it takes to preserve it always," Che' added quietly. "Even my mother understands that now."

"I still cannot believe how easy the transformation was because she now fits perfectly in our family. I cannot picture her not being a part of it," Akeila said softly.

"Some people do not understand the power of love and forgiveness but I am so happy that we did, honey," he murmured.

"I love you."

"I love you, Akeila, always."

Franko got off the phone and gave a victorious laugh. Then he walked to the refrigerator, retrieved a beer, and drank it down very quickly. Everything was going exactly the way that he had planned, and it felt great. He was finally going to avenge his family's death. These past few months he had planned and plotted very carefully to have that accomplished, thanks to the information that Michelle had volunteered. He was very good at executing a plan, which was why the police had never arrested or persecuted him for his shady dealings. The government had been trying for years to convict him for a number of different crimes; selling and trafficking humans and the distribution of narcotics were some of the illegal things that he did. They were unsuccessful in securing convictions because he was always a step ahead of them. The few people that he had working for him were very loyal and were great at what they did. They were always well compensated for their services, and he never made them feel threatened in any way, which was why they enjoyed working for him. Tomorrow he would put his master plan into effect, and his enemy would not see it coming.

"Tomorrow!" he shouted as he walked toward his bedroom, laughing.

CHAPTER 10

Akeila woke up to Link laughing and bouncing on her bed. It was seven in the morning, and she has decided to sleep in late because it was the weekend. During the weekdays getting up early in the morning for work was very tedious, especially because she was pregnant. Che' was a big help with getting Link off for school. Now, all she wanted to do was remain in bed on that cold winter morning, which was impossible when there was a young child around.

"Link, please stop it," Akeila whispered while rubbing her eyes. She was thankful that she had put on a night gown sometime during the night. After making love with her husband, sleep came very easily, but because of her frequent trips to the bathroom throughout the night, she was still very tired.

"Morning, Mommy," Link said while hugging her tightly. Akeila wrapped her arms around her son and smiled; she couldn't be mad at him for long. She then kissed him on his nose.

"I am so hungry," she teased. "I am going to eat you up!" She started nibbling on his tummy playfully.

"Mommy, please don't!" Link said laughing and wiggling.

"Tickle, tickle, tickle!"

"Mom, stop!" he giggled.

"Oh baby," Akeila murmured softly, stopping abruptly as her breathing quickened. "Honey, Mommy has to stop now because she is very tired."

"Are you okay now, Mom?" Link whispered, gently touching her face and looking at her with love and concern.

"Yes, honey, Mommy is okay," Akeila reassured him. "Sometimes your sister moves and stays in the wrong place, making it very difficult for me to breathe."

"Can I feel her, Mommy?" Link asked, resting his small hand on her tummy. "Mommy, she is moving again!"

"Yes, she is very hungry." Akeila smiled as she ruffled his curly hair. Touching her tummy was something that he was always fascinated by, and he did it quite frequently.

"I am hungry too, Mommy."

"Let's get some breakfast, then!"

"Breakfast is served!" Akeila looked up and saw her husband crossing the room with love and admiration on his face as he carried a tray in his hands. She had no idea when he had left the bed.

"Daddy, come and feel the baby move," Link said excitedly.

Che' walked over to the bed and gently placed the tray on the night stand. Then he rested his hand on his wife's tummy. He was always amazed by the way that their daughter moved; it was truly a miracle.

"She is hungry and needs to be fed," Akeila said to the men in her life.

"That's why I brought you breakfast," Che' replied, "in bed."

"Did you bring me breakfast too, Daddy?" Link asked eagerly.

"Yes, I did," Che' answered with a smile. He'd woken up early and wanted to do something nice for his wife. He realized that as the pregnancy progressed, she was having problems sleeping through the night. Breakfast in bed would definitely be a way for her to be off her feet for a little longer. Now it seemed that there was a change of plans and he was very happy to comply. "We are all going to have breakfast in bed this morning: toast, omelet, muffins, fruit, and orange juice."

"Yes, yes!" Link screamed.

The Athien family ate their breakfast while joking and laughing about past and current events. They were interrupted moments later by the ringing of the telephone. Che' picked up the phone and then handed it to Akeila. After talking for a few minutes, she hung it up and quickly got out of bed, rushing into the bathroom with her husband following close behind.

"Honey, can you please dress Link? I have to go to the office for a little while," Akeila said as she hurriedly brushed her teeth.

"Why do you have to go there? It is Christmas Eve," Che' said with a disappointed look on his face. "We were supposed to go shopping for Christmas presents."

"We were going shopping?" she asked while regarding him. "I thought that Link and I were going shopping."

"Well, it was supposed to be a surprise. Why should you two have all the fun?" he replied, still very furious with the situation. He was looking forward to spending the day with his family, but now there would have to be a change of plans.

Akeila saw Che's disappointment and knew that she had to be considerate of his feelings. He'd probably had a difficult time in obtaining the time off from his job in order for him to be with them during the holidays, and she appreciated that gesture greatly. "Baby, someone needs my help for about an hour," she said, softly reaching out to touch his face, which needed to be shaved. "Link and I will meet you at the mall in two hours."

Che' knew that he should be understanding of the situation, and he did not want to argue. Akeila was an excellent therapist, and the love that she had for people made her very exceptional. He admired and respected her for the devotion and dedication that she showed his fellow officers. "Okay, but make it one hour," he joked before pulling her into his arms. "I will have to talk to your supervisor." He kissed her passionately.

Akeila and Link arrived at her workplace one hour later. The huge building was seven stories high and was home to a number of government offices. There was a security guard at the entrance, and the place was under surveillance twenty-four hours a day. Upon entering her office, which was located on the third floor, Akeila walked over to the desk and placed her bag on the table. The office had a very homely feeling that helped her patients to relax and unwind. There were two pieces of art hanging on the walls, two green potted plants in the corner of the room, a recliner, a chair, and a desk with a computer. There was also a toy box in the far corner that was filled with toys, to entertain her son on his frequent trips to the office. The only day of the week when he wasn't there was on Wednesdays because Mrs. Athien picked him up from school.

She looked at her reflection in the bathroom mirror and smile. Her face was glowing from the pregnancy, and it seemed like it was slightly swollen. Her hair had grown a few inches longer and fell over her shoulders. The light makeup that she wore was very natural looking, but the purple lip gloss brought out her luscious lips. She was casually clothed in a pair of maternity jeans and a red cashmere turtleneck sweater that fit over her round tummy. The black blazer, navy blue scarf, and boots made her look very chic.

"Mommy, can I play a game on the computer?" Link asked as she hung their coats on the hanger.

"Yes, you can, but you will have to use my laptop. I have downloaded some educational games for you," Akeila said as she retrieved it from her bag. Over the past few months, Link had been showing a great interest in those games, so she had made them easily accessible to him. She observed him closely as he sat next to his toys and eagerly played the game. She was still bewildered by his astuteness.

A loud knock on the door brought her back to reality. "Come in," she said with a smile on her face.

"Good morning," the patient greeted her. "Please have a sit, Mr. Franko," Akeila said as she sat in her chair. "I was told that you are contemplating suicide and needed an intervention."

Franko regarded Che' Athien's wife for a few seconds and then smiled. For the past few months he had been a patient of hers, coming to see her once a week. His contacts had made it possible for that to happen; they had created false documents stating that he was a veteran. This was very easy to do because his biological father was a retired army general, and they shared the same name. He now understood why Michelle hated the woman. She was intelligent and compassionate in such a unique way that everyone left her sessions with a feeling of importance and purpose. That was truly a gift from God, and he admired that about her. The woman was gorgeous and very sophisticated, and under different circumstances she would have been able to help him deal with some of his emotional scars. He let his eyes wander to where his enemy's son was sitting, and his anger increased considerably because of the child's similarity to Che'. *That bastard has everything—the perfect family, riches, a great job, and an amicable position in society. He does not deserve it.* He looked at Akeila once more and smiled. This was Che' Athien's weak point, and they were at his mercy.

"Have a seat, sir," Akeila said, looking at her patient with uneasy eyes as he remained standing.

Franko slowly reached into his pocket, retrieved a pistol, and pointed it at her. "Sit down, Mrs. Athien, and do not make a sound. If you do, I will not hesitate to shoot your son," he ordered with abhorrence in his eyes.

Upon hearing the threat against her son, Akeila sat abruptly in her chair. This hostile situation was surprising and unbelievable, and fear cripples her heart. She quickly looked at her son, who sat quietly playing his game, unaware of what was going on in his presence. She wanted to shield him from this unforeseen situation. "Please do not hurt my son," she whispered, looking pleadingly at her patient as thoughts of an injured Link filled her mind.

"If you listen and do what you are told, no one is going to get hurt," Franko replied, knowing that he was not telling the truth. He had no problem killing anyone that his adversary loved. She and her son were pawns in the game of destroying Che. "I have no problem with you," he added, sitting on the chair in front of her, still pointing the gun at her.

"Then why are you doing this?" Akeila said quietly, rubbing her tummy gently and trying to calm herself. "My supervisor told me that you needed help. Please let me be at your service."

"That was part of the plan. I do not need your help," he said, emotionless. "In fact, I never did."

"What plan are you talking about?" Akeila asked as she started to panic. She needed to be calm and strong, so she focused on her son and unborn daughter. She then took two long, deep breaths and relaxed a little.

"Listen to a story," he said, staring at her. He then spoke about his sad, abusive childhood and the struggles that his family had to go through. He constantly mentioned the devotion and love of his mother and big brother, to ensure that they were survivors in such a toxic situation. "After a while, things got better. My mom received a small inheritance, and later we got jobs and were finally able to achieve some financial stability. We had businesses, houses, and boats. We were living the English dream . . . until someone came and took everything."

"What does that have to do with me?" Akeila asked.

"Everything," Franko said with rage. "My brother was imprisoned for fraud a few years ago. He committed suicide, and my mother had a heart attack shortly after because she could not deal with the loss of her son."

Akeila observed the man sitting in front of her. Anger, heartlessness, and rage were visible in his actions and on his face. Professionally she could tell that he was beyond her help. He was fully consumed with revenge and hate, and that combination was very lethal and dangerous. She looked at her son again and realized that securing his safety was the greatest importance.

"Che' Athien, your husband took everything from me," Franko yelled, now pointing the gun at Akeila's head. "He took away the only family that I have, and he will pay dearly. I am going to take what's most important to him—you and his son."

"Mommy, Mommy!" Link screamed as he looked at Franko across the room with the gun pointing at his mother.

"Shut that brat up, before I do!" Franko ordered, and he shifted the gun to Link.

"Please let me talk to him," Akeila cried, running to her son without waiting for an answer. She took his frightened body in her arms. "Link, honey, please stop crying. I need you to be strong and do exactly what I tell you." She then whispered something in his ears that was not noticeable to their kidnapper. "Do you understand?" she questioned loudly. "No more crying." She dried his tears and kissed his cheeks.

"Okay, Mommy, I promise," Link murmured softly.

"Enough of this nonsense," Franko shouted from across the room. He couldn't stand watching the love that mother and son shared. He knew that his mom loved him, but she had never looked at him the way that Akeila was looking at her son. One could tell that she would easily give her life for him. "Now we are going to leave this building, and I would appreciate it if you two cooperate. If you don't, I will not hesitate to shoot, and since this gun is a silencer, no one will hear me." He then pushed the gun at Akeila's side, where it was not visible, and grabbed Link by his hoodie.

"Let me hold him," she said angrily, pulling her son and securing him in front of her.

"Now walk slowly and act as normal as possible. Just remember I will shoot if anyone disobeys me," Franko warned.

"We will do whatever you say," Akeila said quietly as they walked toward the elevator on the fifth floor.

The journey to the main entrance of the building seemed to take forever. Akeila was nervy, and her heart was beating very quickly. They did not encounter anyone on the way because it was Christmas Eve; there were only a few employees working that day. She tightly held her son's small shoulders, squeezing very gently at times to reassure him that he would be fine. She would protect him with her last breath, knowing that Franko would have no difficult in killing him. He was a very evil and wicked man, and she would not allow him to harm her little boy. They passed the security guard, who smiled and wished them a Merry Christmas and happy New Year, and then they headed to the entrance.

Now is the time to create a diversion, Akeila thought, and she acted very quickly. It would be her only chance to do so, and she had to take it.

"Ouch," she groaned with agony, holding her tummy. "I think that the baby is coming. It hurts so badly! Oh, please help."

"What? The baby is coming?" Franko asked with a nervous and surprised look on his face as he focused his attention on her.

"I think that my water just broke," she whispered, moaning while rubbing her belly. Franko stared at Akeila and in the process lowered his pistol. As that opportunity presented itself, she stomped her small boot heel forcefully unto his foot, and he jumped in agony.

"Run, Link, run!" she screamed as the boy ran toward where the guard was sitting reading a magazine, oblivious to what was happening.

"That was very stupid!" Franko said. "Now you will have to see your son die." He aimed the gun at Link, who was still running. On impulse, Akeila grabbed his arm and bit into it with all her might, causing him to miss his target.

"You bitch!" he said crossly, yanking his hand away and then punching her in the face before pulling her outside.

"Che'!" Akeila cried as tears rolled down her face.

"He is not here to help you!" Franko yelled. "You need to accept that. Try this again, and I will torture you slowly." He then pushed her into a waiting car and got in beside her.

Akeila sat in the dark car next to her kidnapper, and even though she was petrified, her thoughts were of her son. Was he safe? Did he reach the security guard, and did he do what she has instructed? She wiped away the blood that was dripping from her busted lips. She knew that Franko was quite capable of doing anything. Now that Link was safe, she had to concentrates on protecting her unborn child. It was definitely going to be a difficult task, and she needed her husband more than ever. She placed her hands tenderly around her tummy, shielding the baby against the terror that was about to come.

Che' stood at the entrance of the busy mall and awaited his family's arrival. His security guards were somewhere in the shadows, but it did not concern him. They had done an admirable job of protecting him over the years, and he trusted them wholeheartedly. The weather was very cold, but that did not stop the large amount of shoppers who wanted to do their last-minute shopping. The holiday joy could be felt and seen all around. There were Christmas decorations all over, and old Rudolf and Santa Claus stood a few feet from where he was standing as kids and families tried to get their pictures taken. He could not wait for Link to get here so that they could have their photo taken too. *Where are they?* he wondered while looking at his watch. He realized that they were two hours late. He looked at his image in the store mirror and noticed how impressively he was dressed. The tan sweater, black Ralph Lauren jacket, and tan scarf coordinately perfectly with his black jeans and Prada booths. As he slowly ran his fingers through his thick black hair that had just started to turn grey, two lovely blonde women passed by, smiling flirtatiously at him. He smiled back cautiously in response and walked away. Years ago, this would have been the perfect occasion for him to introduce himself and eventually have company for the rest of the evening. Now he was a very happily married man who desperately needed to be with his family.

He dialed Akeila's number once again. Upon receiving no answer for the sixth time, he started to get an uneasy feeling in his heart. Why wasn't she answering? Most times when she was with a patient, she would not answer her phone, but she always acknowledged his call with a text message. He put the phone back in his pocket and adjusted his gun, which he always carried safely hidden under his jacket. Maybe she decided to go home first. He reached for his phone in order to dial the number but was interrupted by an incoming call.

"Hello?" Che' said curiously, wondering who was calling him on his private line. This number was restricted; only his family and job had it. Knowing that the call was important he waited patiently for the caller to announce himself.

"Mr. Athien, this is the Woodstock Police Department," the caller said. "There is a little boy here stating that he is your son."

"What is his name?" he said, remaining motionless and anxiously waited for the answer. Never in a million years would he have imagined getting a call of this nature. When he heard Link's name, his heart skipped a beat as fear threatened to overtake him. "Is he okay? Where is my wife? I am on my way." Then he rushed to his car with a million questions in his mind. They did not answer the question when he asked about his wife, which led him to believe that something was wrong. There was an uneasy feeling deep in his heart. *Please let them be okay,* he prayed as he sped to the police station. Within minutes he was there.

Che' found his son sitting with a female police officer. The child looked very sad and petrified. His eyes were red, and his small face was stained with tears as he looked toward the entrance of the door. With a heavy heart Che' took Link in his arms. "Oh my son, are you okay?" he whispered ruffling his curly hair.

"Daddy, the bad man got Mommy," Link said, and he started crying again.

"Who got Mommy?" Che' asked while comforting his little boy. The pain that he felt at that moment was stifled with fear as he probed for answered.

"The man in her office had a gun. Mommy told me to run and never look back, and I ran. She injured his foot and bit him, and I saw him hurt Mommy," Link blustered, crying as he concluded.

Che' held his son tightly while the tears fell from their eyes. His worst nightmare had come true. The thought of Akeila and their unborn child injured caused a pain in his heart that he had never before experienced. He had to be strong for them, but for a quick minute he was very weak. He slowly mustered all the strength that he possessed, knowing that leaving without her was not an option. He went to question the police officer that was on duty. He was going to uses all his experience and resources to find her. After informing his employees about the crisis, he contacted his mother, requesting that she come and take Link home. He then collected all the relevant information pertaining to his wife's disappearance. *Who could this man be?* he wondered, *and what does he want with my wife?* She had no enemies to his knowledge. He ordered the surveillance tape from Akeila's workplace to be sent to his office, and he called in some of his best investigators. He was on a mission to find his wife and was not going to fail.

When his mother arrived, he kissed his son good-bye.

"Daddy," Link said softly, "Mommy said to tell you, 'Your biggest fraud case.'"

Che' squeezed Link tightly in his arms, fighting back tears that were threatening to fall once again. "You did great, son, and I am so proud of you. I will bring Mommy home, I promise." He walked up to his mother and hugged her tightly. "Take care of my son."

Mrs. Athien wrapped her arms securely around Che' to comfort him. When she heard what had happened and saw the pain on her son's and grandson's faces, it broke her heart. This was her family, and seeing them in agony brought tears to her eyes because she could feel it too. Over the past few months, she had gotten to know Akeila very well, and she soon realized that her daughter-in-law was a perfect wife and mother. As the days went by she was becoming more fond of her and was greatly looking forward to the birth of her granddaughter. Link was everything that a grandmother dreamed of: he was kind and attentive, always showered her with his love, and asked questions that she loved to answer. He kept her busy and alert, and she loved it. This was her family, and she wanted everyone to be safe. "Be careful, son. Good luck, and please bring Akeila home."

When Che' arrived at his office, his best agents were there working on the tips that they had received from him. Homeland Security had the most efficient equipment in finding and tracing people, and his agents were very intelligent and good at their jobs. The case became top priority. Akeila had given him the most important tip, the fraud case, and as they went through these cases, he thought about her. When the agent showed him the file with his biggest fraud conviction, he knew that they had found his enemy; there was an investigation done on the man before, but without a conviction. The research stated that he and his mother were deceased; the only living relative was a man named Franko, who was a notorious drug lord and criminal but was never caught by the authorities. He gazes at the picture of his adversary on the computer monitor as rage filled his heart. Franko's brother has committed suicide in prison, and the mother died of heart failure shortly after. Che' was fully convinced that Franko's motives were revenge for the loss of his loved ones. He blamed him for their death and used his wife to get to him. *How did he get connected to Akeila?* he wondered. She only counseled war veterans who were referred by the government. *The kidnapper must be getting some inside help,* he rationalized while taking a sip of the cold black coffee that was sitting on his desk. "Who would help that criminal," he said to himself.

He was interrupted by an agent, who brought the video tape from Akeila's building. As the staff carefully examined the tape, they observed Franko entering the building and passing security without being checked. Moments later he emerged with Link and Akeila, and Che's heart skipped a beat when he saw them. He saw how brave she was for their son as he ran away, and he lost it when Franko punched her in the face.

"Bastard!" he yelled taking his pistol and firing at Franco's image on the television monitor. His staff looked at him with surprise and confusion on their faces. They probably thought that he was going crazy, and that may be true. His reputation of thriving under pressure was suddenly threatened by his actions. This was his family that a madman was hurting.

"There are traitors among us assisting Franko with his vendetta against me. Find them!" Che' ordered. "I am going to take care of Mr. Franko my way."

Che' Athien could not get the image of Akeila screaming his name out of his mind. She looked horrified and vulnerable, and as Franko led her away, his heart broke into pieces. He could not lose her. She and his unborn baby needed him, and he was not going to let them down. He then reached into his gun cabinet and took out a Magnum revolver and a .45, loading them with bullets. His nemesis wanted a fight, and he was going to give it to him. This was personal, and no one was going to stand in his way—not the English government or whatever protocol they may use. He was counting on the bastard calling.

Suddenly his cell phone rang, and he glared curiously at it, thinking that this may be the call that he was waiting for. Disappointment filled him when he realized that it was his mother.

"Hello, Mother," Che' said. "How is Link doing?"

"He is asking for you and his mom," she replied softly. "That's not the reason that I called."

"I do not have the time to talk about anything right now. I really have to go," he said, and he was about to hung up the phone.

"Son, I cannot seem to get Michelle out of my mind," Mrs. Athien said quickly with concern in her voice.

"Mom, not now," Che' said indignantly, "My pregnant wife is missing, and you are worried about Michelle?"

"Wait, son! Michelle told me that you and she were getting back together soon. When I told her that this was impossible because you will never leave your wife, she told me that Akeila would be the one leaving."

"Michelle said that?" Che' asked while he tried to place the pieces together.

"Son, I do believe that she knows about what happened to Akeila," Mrs. Athien said with a heavy heart.

"Mother, I am going to send you a picture message. Let Link shows it to you," he said. "Tell me if you have seen this guy with Michelle before."

"Yes, I did," she replied eagerly seconds later. "I had invited her to brunch a few days ago, and he was the one that dropped her off in his car. She did not want me to see who it was, so he quickly drove away."

"Thank you, Mom. You may have just saved my wife's life," Che' said happily.

"Thank your brilliant son, because if he was not here, I would not be able to retrieve that picture message," she replied. "Please bring Akeila home." Then she hung up the phone and looked at her grandson; her heart reached out to him. He sat quietly on the couch and for the first time looked like his young age. He was very sad and missed his mother terribly. He was quite aware that his mother was in danger. Mrs. Athien took him in her arms, singing and rocking him slowly to sleep.

"Put a trace on this number and find out the location of the person immediately!" Che' ordered, and he handed them Michelle's cell phone number. She always had that device with her. He grabbed his jacket and rushed to the door, with two of his best guards following him, fully armed.

CHAPTER 11

The night was terribly cold with darkness all around, and the only visible light was a small crack in the door. There were no signs of life, and if a pin was dropped, the sound would have been heard all around. The only living being present was Akeila Athien, who sat in a dark corner curled up in a ball as she tried to warm herself. She was shivering, and her teeth chattered uncontrollably. Although the leather jacket that she was wearing was lined with lambskin, it was not enough to shield her from the harshness of the cold, heatless room. *Where am I?* she wondered, gazing into the darkness as hunger, thirst, and fright consumed her. She accepted that she had been kidnapped by Franko, but having no idea where he had taken her was terrifying. When he took her, she was blindfolded and had no idea where their destination was. He then brought her to an old cabin, locked her in this dark room, and left. All her pleading and reasoning did not appeal to his conscience as he walked away laughing like someone who was in a trance. How long had she been missing? She knew that by now there were people looking for her. "God, please help me," she prayed. The baby was so quiet that it worried her. "Che, where are you?" She cried as the tears fell from her eyes. "We need you so much right now."

Then she thought of Link, the way that he giggled when she tickled him, his ruffled hair, and his smile. Loving memories of her husband and the love and passion that they shared created a way for her to cope with the suffering that her body was going through. Suddenly she heard footsteps, and her heart skipped a beat. She did not know whether to be relieved or terrified. It was definitely Franko, and she needed food and a blanket even though his cruel intentions were to bring harm on her husband. She looked at the door and waited for her kidnapper to arrive.

Upon entering, he turned on the lights, and Akeila was flabbergasted when she saw his companion. She quickly rubbed her eyes to make sure that they were not deceiving her. Michelle Finn stood before her with a smile on her cold face. She wore a long mink coat with tall leather boots, and long blonde hair hung over her shoulders. Her red lips and smoky eye shadow made her look like Cruella de Vil in the movie *101 Dalmatians*. She was mean and evil as she stood in the doorway.

"Are you cold, Akeila?" she asked before laughing loudly. "That look is very becoming of you—tired and helpless."

"Why isn't there any heat in this room?" Franko asked with a surprised look on his face as he observed his hostage shivering. Seeing her pregnant and suffering reminded him of his mother after her husband beat her, and that appealed slightly to his icy heart.

"What different does it make?" Michelle said callously. "She is going to die anyway."

"That may be, and even though I would like to see her dead, it is not time," Franko said, smiling. "I am going to put the heat on." He hastily left the room.

"Why does every man feel that they have to cater to you?" Michelle yelled angrily at Akeila. "You are *nothing!*" When Akeila remained silent, it upset her anger even more. "Che' should be with me and not you—the house, cars, money, and riches should all be mine!" She allowed her anger to take over. "Even that baby in your tummy should be mine and Che's."

Akeila continued to regard Michelle as she yelled, and she realized that this woman was truly obsessed with her husband. When they'd first met, Akeila's impression of Michelle was that she was beautiful and sophisticated, and Akeila even felt a little intimidated in her presence. However, as she got to know her better, it became obvious that Michelle was a woman scorned. Akeila tried to be friendly and hold a conversation with her but was rewarded with resentment. Michelle was always unpleasant to her by trying to embarrass her at any given chance and by saying unkind things to anyone who would listen. There were times when they were present in the same room, and Akeila would feel Michelle's piercing, hateful eyes on her. She soon realized that the woman loathed her, so she stayed away from her. Che' was a wonderful man, and any woman would love to have him in her life. Akeila could not hate her for wanting him back. Even though Michelle's main purpose in life was to break up her marriage, Akeila never hated her—she pitied her.

"I feel sorry for you," Akeila said softly, looking Michelle directly in her cold eyes. "You are hateful, cruel, and selfish. Your life is like an empty shell, and you are going to die a very lonely woman."

"What did you say, bitch?" Michelle said crossly as she lifted her foot and aimed it at Akeila bulging stomach before launching forward. Akeila grabbed hold of her attacker's foot with all of her strength before it made contact, and she pushed Michelle, who fell and landed on her back.

"Ouch, you bitch!" Michelle cried, quickly getting to her feet. "You are going to pay for that dearly."

"Listen—Che' will never love you. You are a woman of no substance, a washed-up model, and I pity you," Akeila concluded as Michelle turned many different shades of red.

"He will love me again—after you are dead!" she said with venom in her voice. "I hate you with a passion, Akeila, and killing you will be a pleasure."

"Ladies, ladies!" Franco said, entering the room and looking from one to the other while they glared heatedly at each other. He could tell that they were arguing, and he was not in the frame of mind to deal with their pettiness. He wanted Che' Athien to be at his mercy; that was of the utmost importance to him.

"Darling, I need you to kill her right now," Michelle said, smiling seductively at Franko.

"Sorry, not yet," he replied, smiling back at her. "You will have enough time to do whatever your heart desires after I am done with her."

"What do you mean by that? That was our plan!" she said with a confused look.

"That was *your* plan, darling. I need to get my revenge against Che' Athien, and kidnapping his wife was the way to accomplish that," Franko replied, very confident of himself.

"Are you talking about my Che' Athien?" Michelle asked in disbelief, looking at Franko for answers.

"Yes, that one, the bastard!" he replied, glaring at Akeila, who remained quietly sitting in the corner.

"What did he ever do to you?" Michelle tried to place the pieces together now that she was over the shock.

"He took my family away from me!"

"I do not understand. I was not aware that you knew him personally."

"I did not know him until he sent my brother to jail, where he later committed suicide. The pain was too great for my mother, so she had a heart attack a few months later. You, my darling, made it possible for me to get my revenge on that bastard." Franko laughed as he concluded.

"You can't hurt Che'!" Michelle screamed angrily, pushing Franko out of her way. She could not believe what she had just heard. He had used her in a way that no one had done before. What made her mad was the fact that she was clueless to her partner's motives. "You used me, Franko, and you won't get away with that!"

"I will have my revenge, and *no one* is going to stand in my way!" he said heatedly. "I have waited years to get to this point. You and I make an excellent team, so you can either stick to the original plan or leave."

"And miss all the fun?" she said, looking at Akeila, who triggered her anger. She would have to be smart and one step ahead in order to get even with Franko. He had used her to get to the man that she loved, and he would pay dearly. No one was ever going to take Che' away from her!

"That's my girl," Franko said softly, and then he kissed her deeply on the lips.

Akeila gazed at the two people standing in front of her. They were wicked, detestable, and deserving of each other. She listened to their argument and realized that they had no problem using or hurting each other. The look in Michelle's eyes assured her that even though it seemed that she had made peace with him, it was far from over. Suddenly she felt a sharp pain in her tummy. *Oh no, not now,* she thought, pretending that it did not happened. Then it occurred again. She was almost eight months pregnant and needed the baby to wait because there was still a month to go. Her enemies were not mindful of what was going on, because they were still wrapped in each other arms. She certainly did not want her daughter to come into this world surrounding by so much hate.

"Che," she whispered softly to herself. "Baby, we need you so much now."

Franko could not believe what he was hearing, so he pulled himself out of Michelle arms and looked at Akeila. She sat in a corner curled up, cold and weak and hungry, yet she called for her husband. He had tried to put the heat on but was unsuccessful because the cabin was very old, and the heating system was not working. "You are calling for your husband? That bastard!" he said, laughing while removing Akeila's phone from his pocket. "Let's give him a call, then." He dialed the number.

The ground was now covered with snow, and there was a very cold wind blowing that made it very difficult to see. It was about six in the evening and was starting to get very dark as Che' and his men drew close to the location of where Michelle's cell phone signal was. There was no moon in the sky, so they had to use flash lights to observe their surroundings. His team had done a fantastic job at tracing the signal. He was very eager to get to his wife and had a feeling in his heart that she needed him desperately. Sometimes it seemed like he could hear her voice calling out to him. Images of her hungry, cold, and injured kept popping up in his mind, and they gave him the strength and determination to fight harder in finding her. She has been missing for a little over eight hours. Knowing his enemy's profile and Michelle's obsession, catering to Akeila's basic needs would not be of any interest to them. The combination of the two partners in crime was very deadly, and he could not wait to confront and deal with them accordingly. "Hang in there, baby," he whispered softly to himself.

Suddenly his phone rang, and Akeila's name came up on his caller ID. He knew that it was the kidnapper. "Hello?" he said calmly, trying very hard to control his anger.

"Che' Athien," Franko said with confidence in his voice. He had the advantage and was going to make full use of it. The prospect of getting his revenge gave him the gratification of finally having his rival precisely where he wanted him: at his mercy. "I've got your wife, and if you want to see her alive, you will have to do exactly what I order."

"Who are you, and how do I know that she is with you?" Che' asked, acting clueless. He wanted so desperately to hear her voice and find out how she was doing; however, he had to be smart in order to obtain all the information that was needed.

"You will soon know who I am," Franko replied, laughing victoriously as he looked from one woman to the next.

"Can I talk to her? Then I will do as you wish."

"Only for a few minutes." He placed the phone near his hostage's mouth while putting the speaker on.

"Che'?" Akeila said, crying while trying unsuccessfully to be strong. "Honey, I am cold and hungry, and the baby—"

"Shush, don't talk, darling. I love you so much and will never let you down. Remember that, my love," he said softly as tears fell from his eyes. He felt like someone had ripped his heart out his chest, and it was very painful listening to her. "Baby, you have to be strong for me and our daughter."

"Che', I love you, and I will. Link—"

"Okay, that is enough!" Franko interrupted. He was filled with jealousy over the love between husband and wife. All his life, he had never experienced that kind of unconditional love. "Now, listen to what you have to do." He gave his instruction.

Che' and his men began strategizing a plan as soon as he hung up the phone. They had listened to the taped conversation that he had with Akeila, and he was more determined to put an end to the crisis. They were now in close proximity to the cottage and had to figure out a way to enter without being noticed. His wife crying was a force that drove him to work fast and to be successful. He would not let her down, and Franko would not know what hit him. He wanted Che' Athien, and he was going to have him quicker than expected.

The room was quiet. The cottage was cold, and the show was falling consistently against the window. Each occupant was deep in their own thoughts, whether it was of victory, pain, or frustration.

Michelle fixed her eyes on Akeila, who sat quietly in a corner rubbing her tummy. Then she looked at Franko as he played with his pistol. The reality had finally hit her that she had lost the only thing that she had ever wanted, which was Che' Athien and his millions. After listening to the phone conversation between him and Akeila, she was now fully convinced that he would never love in that manner, and it hurt. Franko had used her to get to Che', and she despised him for it. She did not want Che' to die; all she wanted was to marry him and enjoy his millions. When she found out that Akeila was back and was living happily with the man of her dreams, and that they had a son, abhorrence and jealousy took control of her heart. She wanted to get rid of her permanently and had approached her partner in crime, who was more than happy to assist her. They formulated a plot, and she was very pleased to know that success was on the horizon. Akeila would be gone, and she would be there to comfort Che' as he grieved for the loss of his wife. Eventually he would love her again, and they would be a family. She would be a mother to his son, and maybe they would adopt another child. Most important, they would be the power couple among the wealthy, and she could not wait to take her place as mistress of the Athien estate. That was all she had ever wanted.

Franko had capitalized on her passionate and deadly pursuit of Che' to get what he wanted. She thought about all the times that he wanted to obtain information about everything pertaining to the Athien family, and her anger surged. Why didn't she see his motives for doing so? What would Mrs. Athien think? The old woman would never forgive her if she knew of her role in the plot of having her son killed. This was something that she would never allow to happen because her friend had always showed her love and respect. Living without Che' was a future that she was not willing to face. She looked at Akeila once more and comprehended that even though she hated her, she envied her more. That simple woman had everything that she had ever wanted in life, which was Che' Athien and his millions. It hurt even more knowing that he truly loved her. She may have lost Che', but Akeila would never have her happy ending.

"Your husband will take a long time to get here," Franko said to Akeila. "This cabin is a very long drive from the city, and with the large amount of snowfall, it will be difficult to get here. It will be my pleasure to kill your husband because I have waited so long to get my revenge, and now it is finally happening."

"You should not celebrate just yet," Akeila said, breathing heavily as a contraction come upon her. They had been coming more frequently during the past hour, and she knew that she would need medical attention very soon. "My husband is the best at what he does, and he is definitely going to get you."

"Ha! That is wishful thinking on your part, Mrs. Athien," he said confidently. When his nemesis came, he would be prepared to deal with him in the worst way possible.

"Oh, ouch!" Akeila cried out in pain as a contraction came. It was more painful than the previous ones, and she could not stop herself from crying out.

"What is wrong with you?" Michelle asked, wishing that she was far away. Nothing was going the way that she had planned.

"The baby is coming!" Akeila said with tears in her eyes. She felt very weak and helpless for a moment; however, being around these horrible people gave her the determination to be strong.

"Shouldn't we do something to help her, Franko?" Michelle asked, though she didn't really care whether or not he did.

"Did you have a change of heart, my darling?" he asked sarcastically. "Suddenly you are motivated in helping your worst enemy."

"I do not care what happens to that bitch," she shouted resentfully. She may have lost Che', but she was certain that Akeila would not have him, and her death would easily solve that problem.

"You both deserve each other," Akeila said softly when the pain diminished. "You two live your lives full of hate, missing out on all the good things that life has to offer, like love, prosperity, family, and a sense of accomplishment."

"Those things do not matter to me. My revenge is what I live for," Franko replied, laughing. "You may have all those things Mrs. Athien, but you are soon going to die."

"I am not going to die," Akeila said with conviction in her voice. "My husband is going to save me, and guess what, Franco? He is going to do to you so much more than what he did to your weak brother. You and your brother are pathetic people."

"Shut up, you stupid bitch! How dare you speak about my family in that manner!" he yelled. He was consumed with rage and punched Akeila in the face. She screamed and rolled herself into a ball, trying to protect her unborn child. He then pointed the gun at her head with fury blazing in his eyes.

"Why don't you bully someone who can defend himself?" Che' shouted from the front of the room's door, pointing his gun at Franko. When he heard Akeila scream, he launched forward, forgetting the plan that he and his men had formulated. All he knew was that she needed him.

"Well, well, look who showed up!" Franko said with a surprised look on his face. "You got here faster than I had anticipated." He continued to aim the gun at Akeila's head.

"Che'!" Akeila whispered lovingly at her husband as hope entered her heart. She thought that Franko was going to kill her after saying those spiteful things to him, but Che' had come in the nick of time to rescue her. She was in a lot of pain, and her contractions were now only minutes apart. "Oh no," she murmured as her water broke, gushing down her leg and into her boot.

"Are you okay, Akeila?" Che' asked gently, still pointing his pistol at Franko. When he entered the room and saw her battered and bruised, he wanted desperately to take her in his arms and take away all the pain. His anger intensified, and he focused on Franko once more; he had no problem killing this man.

"My water just broke—I think the baby is coming!" she replied, softly breathing in deeply and knowing that she had to stay calm and keep the baby inside a little longer, if she could.

"How does it feel to see the one that you love in pain, helpless, and you can't do anything to help?" Franko asked. "That is the way that I felt when you took my brother away from me."

"Your brother was not helpless," Che' pointed out. "Do you know the amount of families that he cheated from their life savings and retirement? People trusted him with their children's college funds and investments, and he deprived them of it. He was a criminal, just like you."

"Shut up you bastard! You know *nothing* about my brother," Franko shouted angrily. "My brother was a hero."

"Hero? Are you crazy? Look at you, Franko: kidnapping and torturing helpless women and kids. You and your brother kill, steal, and hurt people. You both are evil, pathetic human beings." Che' was trying to get him mad so that he would lose his concentration, and then Che' can make his move.

"Lower your gun!" Franko yelled, totally consumed with anger, "Or I will shoot your wife."

"Che'," Michelle interrupted, "Do as he says." She had remained quiet, trying not to bring attention to herself as she thought of a way to benefit from that situation. By showing concern for Akeila with Che' present, it may give her a second chance with him after Franko killed Akeila. She was praying that he would shoot the woman.

"Why should I take any advice from you, Michelle?" Che' asked, not taking his eyes of his enemy. "You are evil like Franko, and you're one of the biggest mistakes of my life. I regret the time that I have spent in your company. You are a sorry excuse for a woman, and you do not exist to me anymore."

"Please don't say that, Che'! You know that I love you. I am so sorry!" she pleaded, running close to him. "I did not know that he wanted to kill you, darling." When she looked into his eyes and saw the disgust, it finally dawned on her that she had lost him forever.

"Lower your pistol, Che'!" Franko screamed once again. "Or else I am going to shoot your wife."

"I will not," Che' said stubbornly. "If you shoot her, I will shoot you." He had used that tactic many times in the past, and it always worked.

"Ha! Do you think that I care if you shoot me? At least I will take what you love the most before it happens. The fact that you are living without the love of your life would be my revenge, and that's good enough for me."

Che' looked at his wife and could tell that she was in a lot of pain, although she was trying to be brave. She looked so helpless and vulnerable, and he couldn't live without her. It would be better if he was the one to die in her place, because Link and the baby needed her.

"Okay," Che' said softly, lowering the gun as he look at his wife. "Akeila, be strong and know that the best days of my life were what I have spent with you and our son. You are my heart, and I will love you forever."

"Che' baby, I love you," Akeila whispered with tears rolling down her face.

Franko laughed triumphantly and then pointed the firearm at his rival. "Good-bye, you bastard." He cocked the gun as he spoke.

Images of her husband dying in front of her and living a life without him flooded Akeila's mind. She refused to live without him, and their marriage vow of "till death do us part" sang in her heart. She mustered up all the strength that her weak body possessed and launched forward, pushing Franko in the back of his knees. He lost his balance, and the pistol went off, missing its target. Akeila then lost consciousness and fell to the ground.

Che' realized what Akeila was about to do, so he reached for the pistol that was hidden in his boot and fired two shots into Franco's body. His only concern was for his wife, whose body lay lifeless on the ground. He then rushed forward and lifted her protectively in his arms. "Akeila, baby, please open your eyes!" he cried.

CHAPTER 12

Akeila was in and out of consciousness as she heard Che's voice begging her to stay with him. She was fighting desperately to obey him and stay alive, but it was so difficult. She felt very weak, and there was so much pain. She heard sirens and other voices that she did not recognize. *Oh God, the baby is coming. Push!* her mind told her, and she pushed. Then she was out again.

"Akeila, please open your eyes," Che' pleaded. They had arrived at a nearby hospital a few hours ago, and even though she was receiving excellent care from the best doctors available, she was still in a lot of pain. A specialist now sat at his wife bedside. The nurses had informed him that she had lost a lot of blood, which was not a good sign.

"Che'!" Akeila cried softly as she looked at him with weak eyes. "I am . . ."

"Hush, honey," he said while holding her cold hands.

"I am so weak . . . Don't think that I can do this. Something is wrong with the baby."

"Yes, you can do it. Our daughter, Link, and I are counting on you," Che' answered. He looked at his wife, and his heart reached out to her. She looked so small and helpless. He sank down on the edge of the bed, his dark head dropping into her hands. "Please don't leave me, Akeila," he cried as tears ran down his face. "What am I going to do without you?"

"Mr. Athien," the doctor said softly from the front of the room. "You need to go outside so that we can examine your wife."

"I am *not* leaving her," he yelled, angrily holding unto her hand.

"Doctor, please give me a minute with him," Akeila said softly as she looked at her husband weeping. She had never seen him cry before and knew that he was hurting. She wanted to comfort him but was too weak.

"What can I do to make your pain go away?" Che' asked her.

"Kiss me and tell me that you love me."

Che' gently placed his mouth over hers as they gained strength from each other. She grabbed his hand tightly as a contraction rushed over her body.

"Doctor!" he screamed, and they rushed into the room. He stepped aside, giving the doctors and nurses access to his wife. They ordered him to leave the room.

Che' waited outside of the room for what seemed like hours, and paced up and down the hallway. He could not visualize a life without Akeila in it. He felt so helpless and wished that he was in her place.

Mrs. Athien walked up to her son and wrapped her arms around him. His security guards, who were like friends to him, had called and informed her that he was in the hospital with his wife and needed some support. Her heart broke when he remained in her arms sobbing. The last time she remembered seeing him cry was at his father's passing when he was very young.

"I cannot lose her, Mother," he wept. "She is everything to me."

"I know," she whispered, fighting back her own tears. From the moment that Akeila had been kidnapped, she came to the realization that her family couldn't function without the girl. Her grandson and son needed her, and she most definitely did too. Akeila Athien was the catalyst of the Athien family.

"Mr. Athien," the doctor said softly. "Your wife has lost a lot of blood, and the baby is breech. She has been in labor for many hours, and if we cannot change the baby's position and stop the bleeding, we could lose them both. A cesarean section would be our last resort."

"Doctor, please do not let my wife die," Che' pleaded, grabbing his arm.

"I will do my best, and you have to be strong. After all that your wife has been through, she is still fighting. Fight with her, because she still have a lot of fighting to do," the doctor said.

Che' bent over his wife's frail body and kissed her deeply and quickly. He smiled and held her small hand, gazing deeply into her brown eyes. "I love you, and Link and I will be waiting for you."

"Link?" she whispered softly, thinking of her son. He would be lost and devastated without her because of the close relationship that they shared. For the first three years of his life, she had been both parents to him. She would have to fight very hard in order to stay with her family. "I love you too."

Moments later, Che' called his in-laws in Grenada, informing them of what was happening. He needed prayers and support from the people who loved her so dearly. They were the ones who gave him the courage to be strong for the family, and he could not let them down.

Perspiration ran down Akeila's face, and a nurse wiped it away. She was surrounded by doctors and nurses, and from the look on their faces, she knew that time was running out. She was very weak, tired, and in a lot of pain. *I can do this,* she reasoned as thoughts of her baby boy, her unborn daughter, and how much they needed her came to mind. She relaxed, breathed in, and then pushed with all the strength that her weak body possessed as her contraction peaked. Then she focused on her husband's face and memories of the first time they fell in love, their beautiful wedding ceremony, and when they found each other again. How she loved him and the life that they'd made together. She cried out his name when the next sharp spasm caught her.

At the sound of Akeila screaming his name, Che' launched forward and stood motionless, looking at the room. Then he heard her calling his name again and was about to rush forward when his mom caught his arm.

"Son, don't go. You will only be in the doctor's way. Just give them the time that they need to work," she cautioned gently. She hated seeing her son so scared and helpless. He had joined the army at a very young age and was always very strong and brave. At first she was always worrying about him, but because of his strength and self-confidence, the distress was minimized. These qualities help shaped him into an excellent government operative. However, being a husband and father had brought out feelings that she would have never associated with him.

It was Christmas morning, and the hospital was now very quiet. The few staff members that passed by had offered holiday cheers; most were not aware of the agony that the Athien family was going through. It was definitely a white Christmas; even though the snow has stopped falling, it was present all over.

Che' paced the floor once more and then went to a chair to sit, resting his elbows on his knees. Doubt and fear crippled him as he waited. *What is going on?* he wondered. The place was now very quiet. Did he lose her? How would he and Link survive without her? Then he looked up and saw the doctor walking toward him, and he jumped up. They secured a private ward quite easily because of his family's influence. Following him was a nurse carrying a baby wrapped in a blanket.

"Mr. Athien, this is your daughter," the doctor said as they handed the baby to him. Che' took the baby gently and stared at her face, which was perfect. She was healthy and had her mother's round face.

"Doctor, how is my wife?" he asked with concern in his voice. He was very happy to see his daughter, but he wanted desperately to know how her mom was doing.

"She has lost a lot of blood and is sleeping right now. We have given her a blood transfusion and are waiting for her to wake up. I have never seen a patient fight so hard to stay alive. I believe that she will be all right."

When Akeila opened her eyes, she was in a white room that was very clear and pure like snow. *Am I in heaven?* she wondered. Her eyes looked around the quiet room slowly as they adjusted to the lighting. Then she saw Che' sitting in a chair next to her bedside, fast asleep. He looked so tired yet handsome in a rugged way, and his face needed to be shaved. She reached out her hand and touched her husband, her soul mate, and her one true love.

"Akeila, baby, you are awake!" Che' said, smiling and taking her in his arms as tears fell from his eyes.

"Shush, I am okay now," she whispered while crying too.

"You gave me quite a scare."

"What happened? I can only remember bits and pieces."

"You were dehydrated and had high blood pressure, a head injury, and a lot of blood loss. The baby was breech. Everyone thought that you weren't going to make it," he concluded.

"Che', the baby—is she okay?" Akeila asked with concern in her voice.

"Our daughter is doing fine," he replied, smiling as he thought about the bundle of joy that had greeted him earlier.

"Can I see her?" she asked with excitement in her eyes.

"In a few minutes, but first I need to talk to you," Che' replied with a sad look in his eyes. "Akeila, I thought that I had lost you, and I do not know what I am going to do if something like that ever happens again. It could."

"What are you talking about?" Akeila asked. "Women have babies all the time." While looking at his sad expression, she realized that this conversation would not be a good one.

"You were kidnapped and hurt, and because of that you went into premature labor and almost died. The only reason that happened was because of me," he said, not able to look at her.

"Che' Athien, I—"

"Please let me finish," he interrupted. "When you were lying there, I had some time to think about you, Link, and the baby, and I decided what was best for everyone. My life is too dangerous. I have enemies all over the world who are convinced that they can use any of my loved ones to get to me." Che' sighed deeply, still not looking at her as he spoke. "I think that it is best if I leave our family."

"Che' Athien, that the most selfish thing that I have ever heard," Akeila shouted in disbelief. She could not understand why he would ever consider such an idea. "Look at me!" She grabbed him by his hand as he gazed into her big brown eyes. "It was because of you, your love, and the future you had promise me and our children that I survived all of this. I cannot and will not imagine a future without you in it. Where you go, I will go; if you go through the fire, I will be right there beside you, holding your hand. You are my heart."

"I am sorry, Akeila," he cried softly. "I cannot lose you."

"You, my darling husband, will never lose me," she said, wrapping her arms around his waist as they cried together, releasing all the pain and frustration that they had endured over the past two days.

Moments later Che' bought the five-pound, nine-ounce baby girl to his wife, who gazed lovely at her. Even though the baby was eight weeks early, she was in good health. She had drunk a little of her mom's fluids because of her long stay in the tummy, after her water had broken, but she was treated.

"Che', she is perfect and beautiful," Akeila whispered while staring at her daughter, who played with her fingers.

"Just like her mommy."

"Please, honey. I know that I look like a mess."

"A hot mess—*my* hot mess," Che' said as he looked at her with those dark, fathomless eyes that she could read so well. She blushed.

"Mommy, Mommy! You are better now!" Link screamed, rushing into the room and into his mother's arms.

"Link, my special boy! I am so happy to see you," Akeila cried as Che' quickly took the baby from her. He knew that they shared a very special bond and was very happy to bring them together. His mom had informed him that over the past two days, Link had not eaten any of the food that she'd given him, and he cried a lot.

"Are you still hurt, Mommy?" he asked, looking at the tubes that were still attached to her hands.

"No, honey, I am okay now. Thanks to you, my brave knight, Daddy was able to find me sooner."

"Daddy, can I see my sister now?" Link asked as he remained in his mother's arms.

"Yes, you can," Che' replied, and he carried the baby and sat next to his wife on the bed.

"She is so tiny, Mommy," Link whispered while they gazed in admiration at the newest member of the family.

Mrs. Athien stood outside her daughter-in-law's room, not wanting to intrude. They looked so happy even though these past forty-eight had been so trying. She saw them in pain, scared, and helpless, and she concluded that they shared a love and bond that was unique and that only a few people experienced. She was very wrong about so many things, and she greatly needed forgiveness.

"Mother, please join us," Che' said, walking up to her and handing her the baby.

Mrs. Athien gently took the baby in to her arms and stared lovingly at her. Her granddaughter was beautiful and flawless. She now had two lovely grandchildren who gave her a reason to live, thanks to her son and the woman lying on the bed. "I am so sorry, Akeila, for the way that I treated you when you first came into my family. I was wrong and hope that one day you can forgive me," she cried.

"It's over, Mother, and I have already forgiven you. You raised a wonderful son who makes my life complete. I can never hold animosity in my heart for you," Akeila replied. "The information that you gave helped save my life, and I will always be grateful to you. We can now be the family that we were meant to be, unique and loving."

"You called me Mother," Mrs. Athien whispered in disbelief, looking at her daughter-in-law as tears fell from her eyes while her son and grandson looked on.

"Yes, I did," Akeila said, laughing. "Now, you can enjoy your grandchildren, Link and baby Sophia, who was named after you, mom. They are the new generation of the Athien family." Mrs. Athien handed the baby to her son and then took her daughter-in-law into her arms, still crying.

"Grandma, why are you crying?" Link asked, looking at her with a puzzled look.

"I am so happy, my boy," she answered, wiping her tears.

"Okay, Grandma. We are all happy!" he said, and they laughed.

Akeila looked her husband and smiled as he gazed adoringly at her. It felt as though she could read his mind, which was filled with gratitude and everlasting love. This was their family, and it may be unique and different, but it was brought together by love. The struggles that they had been through only made them love and appreciate each other more. Like the old cliché said, "What doesn't break you makes you stronger."

CHAPTER 13

"Ladies and gentlemen, you are invited to the grand formal dinner and dance at the Athien Family Ballroom. The room was donated by Sophia Athien in order to introduce her family to the world."

Akeila stood in front of the huge bedroom mirror wearing only black lace garters and matching bra and panties, examining her body. She was amazed by how fast the postpregnancy weight had come off. Her husband and personal trainer were very firm and determined as they pushed and motivated their student in accomplishing her goal. She was now getting ready for the dinner and dance that was given in her honor. As the season changed from winter to early spring, so did life at the Athien estate. The relationship between Akeila and her mother-in-law was wonderful. She was educated on the history of the Athien family and the role of the mistress of the estate. Secret family recipes were imparted, and all of the old knowledge was passed down as they spent lots of time enjoying each other's company.

The kids made it even more special. Link was an excellent big brother to his four-month-old sister Sophia, who looked like her mother more and more each day. Shortly after the kidnapping, Link was very clingy and did not want to be away from her, but with communication and the reassurance that she was safe, things went back to normal.

Che' continued to do an excellent job as chief of Homeland Security. He later weeded out all the traitors that were involved in the kidnapping. Akeila learned that Michelle had been shot in the back and was now crippled. The bullet that Franko had meant for Che' had shot her instead. She now lived in a nursing home in shame, because her reputation, which was her most prized possession, had been tarnished. Pictures and information of her conspiring to kill the chief of Homeland Security's wife were plastered all over the news. As for Franko, after suffering multiple bullet wounds, he was hospitalized and now sat in prison waiting for trial. Homeland Security had been working very hard to convict him for some of the crimes that they had investigated where he was the prime suspect. Together with the kidnapping and the intent to murder, he would definitely be in prison for a very long time.

Che' walked out of the shower with a towel wrapped around his waist. When he saw his wife scantily clad and applying makeup to her face, he paused because her beauty took his breath away. She was desirable, her petite body was a little curvier, and her breasts were slightly bigger because of the birth of their daughter. Oh, how much he wanted her and missed their intimacy. They had not made love since she'd had the baby, and his body was acing for her. It was very hard at times, especially lying close to her every night and not being able to do anything. Cold showers and fantasies of the time when he would be able to do so helped ease his sexual frustration. He stood motionless, looking at her ripe breasts covered in lace, and he let his eyes wander to her flat tummy and then to her toned legs, which stood firmly in black high heel shoes. He looked at her flawless face, which was perfectly made up, and her long, curly hair fell over her shoulders. His eyes traveled down her body once more and stopped between her legs. His erection was now pointing in front of him as he feasted on her beauty.

Akeila saw her husband staring at her with desire in his black eyes, and she smiled. She knew that the time had arrived for them to glory in each other's bodies once again. A trip to the doctor's office earlier in the day assured her that it was now okay to do so. She wanted to wait after the party to express her love to him, but given the look on his face, she could not deny him any longer.

"Honey, can you please help me with this necklace?" Akeila asked loudly, pretending that she had not seen him standing there.

"Sure, baby," Che' answered hoarsely, walking up and retrieving the necklace from her fingers. He tried very hard not to be affected by her smell and the feel of her skin on his fingers, but it was difficult. Her hair and body had an invigorating aroma of floral and a luminous, creamy touch that he always loved. He wanted very much to replace his fingers with his lips. "All done," he murmured with passion in his voice.

"Thank you," she said, smiling seductively up at him. When he did not move, she added, "Do you want me to thank you properly, darling?" Before he could answer, she slowly reached up and kissed his cheeks lightly before walking away. Che' quickly grabbed Akeila by the arm, turned her to face him, and then gently touched her cheeks and eyebrows. When his fingers caressed her lips, she opened her mouth and sucked on them.

"Baby," he groaned, bending his head and kissing her passionately. She opened her mouth, welcoming his kisses. Che' began moving his hand over her body as they kissed hungrily. He then caressed her lower back and lowered his hand to her buttocks, lifting one of her legs gently while she pulled his towel off and letting it fall to the ground. His erection was quite visible. She caressed his back as his tongue traveled from her mouth to her neck and then her breast. He sucked, nibbled, and bit gently on them as she moaned in pleasure.

"Akeila, baby, we have to stop because I do not want to hurt you," Che' whispered with passion in his voice, pulling away. "If I do not stop now, it will be impossible for me to do so." He looked into her brown eyes, which were filled with passion and desire, and hugged her tightly.

Akeila smiled at him. "Che', this morning I went to the doctor, and he said that it is safe, so we can make love."

"Really?" He smiled, picked her up quickly, and walked over to the bed. He then sat with her on his lap as she gazed lovely at him. He gently stroked her lips and the edge of her jaw. She lifted her hands to the back of his neck and ran her fingers through the hair at the base of his head. He kissed her quickly and then slowly began running his tongue down her neck and then to her breasts, licking, kissing, and sucking as her nipples rose. He laid her on the huge bed, and she spread her legs, wanting him to fill her as her desire for him blossomed. He bent over and took her breasts in his mouth once more while his fingers found her warm, moist womanhood. His lips traveled downward, caressed her bellybutton, and then reached her famine core. He nibbled and sucked as his tongue pleasured her. Akeila trembled and cried out in pleasure, lifting herself upward and wanting him to enter her badly.

"Che," she moaned, "Baby, please."

"I love you, Akeila," he groaned hoarsely with desire as he positioned himself above her. He entered her slowly, plunging into her deeper and deeper as she wrapped her legs around him, bringing him closer.

"Che," she moaned, digging her fingernails in his back and climaxing. She then grabbed hold of his waist, wanting to pleasure him also. She rolled over quickly so that she was now on top of him. "I love you too, Che," she said as she moved her waist rhythmically, lifting herself in and out before going deeper on his shaft. He grabbed hold of her breasts tightly, and passion filled him. She rode him until they both climaxed, screaming each other's names.

"I will love you forever, Akeila Athien," he whispered, looking deeply into her brown eyes.

"We are destined to be together, Che," she said. "Forever my love, forever." She nuzzled into his arms.

The ballroom was filled with elegance and style for the once-in-a-lifetime event. Beauty and vitality contributed to the festive atmosphere. The receptionist table and serving area were decorated with the finest crystal and eating utensils. Bouquets of carnations added to the decorations, and luxury could have seen all around. Akeila walked into the ballroom dressed in a lovely Vivienne Westwood gown. The strapless silk red dress was well designed and chic, and it hugged her body tightly before falling to the ground in a small trail. She was amazed by how lovely the place looked, from the decoration to the distinguished guests. The prime minister other government officials, dukes and duchesses, and other members of high society were present, causing Akeila to be a little nervous. She reached out and held her husband hand tightly as he stood at her side.

Che' smiled lovingly, his eyes reassuring her that everything would be all right. He was handsomely dressed in a white tuxedo with a silk navy blue shirt and black shoes. His daughter, pretty in pink, lay in his arms. Akeila looked around carefully as her eyes searched for the familiar faces of the people that she loved. Then she saw them. Her family had flown in from Grenada to celebrate with her. She quickly walked over to them with Link by her side. He rushed forward, and she noticed how fine looking he was while wearing his white tuxedo. She hugged and kissed her parents and then her sisters, Tasha and Pam. With her confidence intact, she walked back and stood proudly by her husband's side. She looked at him once more and then at their daughter and son, who held on tightly to her hand.

"Ladies and gentlemen, distinguished guests, friends and family, welcome!" Mrs. Athien said to everyone. The turquoise formal dress that she wore made her look much younger. Her hair was formally pinned in a bun, and white shoes and a purse completed up her outfit. She was very happy because of her family. The love and respect that she had for them was felt all around. Her grandchildren were her main topic of conversation, and she spent a lot of time playing with them. Akeila was a wonderful daughter-in-law, and she now fully understood why her son loved her so much. Che' Athien was every mother's dream: he was a wonderful son, husband, and father. They had brought so much joy into her life, and she wanted the world to know. That was why the dinner and dance was a good idea.

"I would like to present to you my wonderful son, Che' Athien; my lovely daughter-in-law; and my grandchildren, Link Seamos Athien and Sophie Athien. They are the future of the Athien family."

Akeila walked toward her mother-in-law and hugged and kissed her. The rest of the family followed while the crowd cheered. She looked at her husband, and they gazed at each other with eyes that were filled with everlasting love.

S ally McGuire have written many short stories during her school years and always keeps a journal. Her love and interest in historical researches of different cultures have earned her an award for excellent in that area. She is a great believer in true love which motivates her to write about it. "Destine To Love" is the first novel that she have written. Sally lives in New York with her son.

CPSIA information can be obtained at www.ICGtesting.com
Printed in the USA
BVOW02s2305270813

329567BV00001BA/4/P